ARA
An Arabian mosaic
: short stories by

AN ARABIAN MOSAIC

Also by DALYA COHEN-MOR

Yusuf Idris: Changing Visions (1992)
Yusuf Idris: The Piper Dies and Other Stories (1992)

AN ARABIAN MOSAIC

*Short Stories by
Arab Women Writers*

Collected and Translated
by
DALYA COHEN-MOR

Potomac, MD, U.S.A.

Sheba Press, P.O. Box 59637
Potomac, MD 20859-9637 U.S.A.

© Dalya Cohen-Mor 1993

First published 1993

All rights reserved. No part of this publication may be reproduced, stored in a retrieval system, or transmitted in any form, or by any means, electronic, mechanical, photocopying, recording or otherwise, without prior permission of Sheba Press.

Cataloging-in-Publication Data available upon request from Library of Congress

ISBN 1-880613-08-5 (cloth)
ISBN 1-880613-06-9 (pbk)
LC No. 92-080017

Manufactured in the United States of America

To Shani

Contents

Acknowledgments	ix
Introduction	xi
The Breeze of Youth *Ulfa al-Idilbi*	1
A Mistake in the Knitting *Ihsan Kamal*	11
My Wedding Night *Alifa Rifaat*	23
Tears for Sale *Samira Azzam*	33
The Future *Daisy al-Amir*	41
The Persian Rug *Hanan al-Shaykh*	49
The Picture *Nawal al-Saadawi*	57
The Picture *Latifa al-Zayat*	65
The Picture *Layla al-Uthman*	77
The Lady with the Story *May Ziyada*	85

Contents

I Want Him a Free Man *Layla Bin Mami*	95
Where To? *Kulit Suhayl al-Khuri*	101
The Cat *Layla Baalbakki*	107
The Cat, the Maid, and the Wife *Daisy al-Amir*	115
A Woman Worth Less than Nothing *Hayat Ibn al-Shaykh*	121
Half a Woman *Sufi Abdallah*	127
A Man and a Woman *Rafiqat al-Tabia*	135
Another Scarecrow *Ghada Samman*	141
The Second and the Truth *Khayriyya al-Saqqaf*	155
Fragments from a Life *Sharifa al-Shamlan*	159
Pharaoh Is Drowning Again *Sakina Fuad*	163
Biographical Notes	173

Acknowledgments

This work has evolved over the period of time in which I taught Arabic literature at the State University of Amsterdam in the Netherlands. The contact with students, and the general observation that women's life in Arab society is often stereotyped and poorly understood provided the first impetus to study and collect stories by and about women from different parts of the Arab world.

I want to thank Professor M. Woidich for welcoming me to his department and providing the fertile environment for the development of this work. As might be expected, it was not always possible to locate and communicate with the authors whose stories are included in this anthology. I want to thank the authors who have responded to my requests and have given me permission to publish translations of their writings. Finally, my thanks go to my husband, Michael, for his enthusiastic support throughout the stages of this project, and for his many insightful suggestions.

I dedicate this book to my daughter, Shani, whose determination to combine a scientist's career with a woman's life has been a source of inspiration to me.

Introduction

RHYTHMS OF REPETITIVE CYCLES IN NATURE REVEAL the latter's innate force and vitality. Human life on earth is primarily manifested in its cycle of re-emergence through birth, childhood, adulthood, middle age, and old age. At the heart of this ongoing life cycle we find the pivotal role of women. In civilized societies, women frequently have to contend with their culture's interpretation of the uniqueness of their biological rhythms, which may either accentuate or mask their pivotal role. In Arab society, this interpretation has set women in a world apart, which often entails segregation, veiling, and divorce from public life. However much they are hidden, rhythms of feminine existence and creativity cannot be suppressed, and they continue to emerge in a variety of forms: art, dance, music, and literature. In the domain of writing, literary rhythms are a reflective pulse of women's consciousness and being. Like biological rhythms they may be overshadowed by the cultural environment and not immediately apparent, but their presence, and the manifestations of their presence, are undeniable.

The stories collected here are by twenty contemporary women writers from different parts of the Arab world. These multiple voices articulate the female experience over the past half-century in regions that range from the

An Arabian Mosaic

Middle East through Arabia to North Africa. They speak of old values and new needs, of marriage, divorce, childbearing, love, sexuality, education, work, and freedom. They explore the male-female dynamics of their societies and question traditional concepts and bequeathed customs as they assert their own desires and aspirations. And they take a stand, be it romantic, conservative, rebellious, moderate, or even radical. The resulting portrait is a colorful mosaic, which is as important as it is endlessly fascinating.

Who are these writers?

They are women of the middle and upper classes whose economic security has afforded them the education and free time needed to write fiction. In a developing world where illiteracy is still widespread and where the overwhelming majority of women are preoccupied with "doing daily battle," Virginia Woolf's basic assumption that "a woman must have money and a room of her own if she is to write fiction"[1] is highly pertinent. The critic who is quick to dismiss Arab women writers as a minority, an educated elite, must be reminded, in Woolf's words, that "fiction, imaginative work, that is, is not dropped like a pebble upon the ground, as science may be; fiction is like a spider's web, attached ever so lightly perhaps, but still attached to life at all four corners. . . . These webs are not spun in mid-air by incorporeal creatures, but are the work of suffering human beings, and are attached to grossly material things, like health, and money, and the houses we live in. . . ."[2]

However, economic freedom does not necessarily entail intellectual freedom. Arab women who are fortunate enough to be able to engage in writing still have to face

Introduction

social opposition to their work, and may even find it impossible to publish it or acquire a readership. The physician and writer Nawal al-Saadawi, a leading Egyptian feminist, first published her study *Woman and Sex* in Egypt in 1972. It caused such an uproar that she was dismissed from her job and had to take refuge in Lebanon. The book, reprinted in Beirut in 1973 and 1974, deals candidly with taboos surrounding female sexuality, such as virginity, circumcision, crimes of honor, and arranged marriage. The Lebanese fiction writer Layla Baalbakki published a collection of short stories entitled *A Spaceship of Tenderness to the Moon* in Beirut in 1963. Nine months later the Lebanese vice squad visited every bookstore that carried her book, and all remaining copies were confiscated. She was then brought to trial on charges of obscenity and harming public morality.[3] The charges were based on her title story, which allegedly contained an "erotic" description of a couple in a love scene. Although Layla Baalbakki was acquitted, she has published little since. Another woman writer, the Egyptian Alifa Rifaat, was discouraged from writing first by her father, then by her husband, and initially had to publish her work under a pseudonym.

The Egyptian male critic Yusuf al-Sharuni, who in 1975 edited the first anthology of Arab women writers, entitled *The 1002nd Night,* offers the following explanation of this state of affairs in the introduction to that book: "Man, especially in our Middle Eastern milieu, does not object to woman's emergence into public life in order to work alongside him, especially if this work relieves him of the burden of bearing the living costs of the family by himself. But beyond that he strongly objects to her having an independent social existence, just as he totally refuses the idea of the home becoming a secondary job for her, subordinate to her outside, wider world. In other words, man still asserts that the home, not external society, is a woman's domain."[4]

The female sociologist Fatima Mernissi has another explanation. In her collection of interviews with Moroccan women, entitled *Doing Daily Battle,* she writes about her experiences "as a Moroccan woman who uses writing and analysis—two tools which are exclusively male in our culture. And let no one tell me that in our heritage there have been women scholars."[5] Mernissi reveals, with an engaging sense of humor, that she has learned to distinguish "the varieties of terrorist tactics that men, who monopolize the symbolic values of our society, use to stop me from expressing myself, or to denigrate what I say—which comes to the same thing."[6] Mernissi identifies two such "terrorist tactics": "Firstly, 'What you are talking about is an imported idea' (referring to access to the cultural heritage); and secondly, 'What you are saying is not representative' (referring to access to science)."[7] As a result, Mernissi discovers that "the relations between the sexes are always inextricably and unconditionally linked to class relations."[8]

Although Arab women writers face restrictive conditions that put extra difficulties in the path of their careers, they nevertheless continue to find a literary outlet for their feelings and thoughts. In the relatively young tradition of short-story writing, which Arab women began to cultivate about half a century ago, there has been a remarkable development in theme, form, and technique[9] since the pioneering work of the Palestinian

Introduction

May Ziyada (1895–1941), and the dedicated efforts of both the Syrian Ulfa al-Idilbi (b. 1912) and the Palestinian Samira Azzam (1927–1967)—the first Arab women writers to devote themselves exclusively to this genre. Two groups of women writers can be distinguished in this anthology: those from the Arab East (*Mashriq*) and those from the Arab West (*Maghrib*). Historically and culturally, these parts of the Arab world have developed differently. For one thing, while the countries in the Arab East were largely under British colonial rule (e.g., Egypt, Palestine, Iraq), the countries in the Arab West (e.g., Algeria, Tunisia, Morocco) were mostly occupied by the French. French rule explains the problem of biculturalism that writers from North Africa face.[10] Whereas British colonial policy did not impose the English language and culture on the colonized, the French embarked on an aggressive linguistic and cultural campaign that sought to replace the indigenous cultures with a French one. The result has been the emergence of whole generations of intellectuals who know little or no Arabic and therefore have to express themselves in French. Examples of such individuals are the Algerian women writers Jamila Debeche and Assia Djebar, and their male compatriots Mohammed Dib and Kateb Yacine, or again the Moroccan novelist Driss Chraibi.[11] Moreover, even the writers who have acquired the Arabic language through the process of Arabization often display a distinct French influence in their writing. For instance, in the story "The Downfall of Waiting" (Casablanca, 1975) the Moroccan writer Khanata Bannuna uses the phrase *'ilab al-layl* to mean "night clubs,"

An Arabian Mosaic

which is a word-for-word translation from the French "boîtes de nuit." (The usual Arabic expression for "night club" is "malha layl"). On the whole, while the majority of literary works coming from the Arab East are in Arabic, those coming from North Africa are in French. In this anthology there are three representatives from North Africa: Rafiqat al-Tabia (Morocco), Layla Bin Mami (Tunisia), and Hayat Ibn al-Shaykh (Tunisia)—all of whom write in Arabic.

The Arabian Peninsula has always been a stronghold of conservative Arab-Muslim values and a firm follower of patriarchal patterns of control over women. The Peninsula was never colonized and throughout the centuries remained resistant to influences from the outside as well as to social change. This background explains why new opportunities for women have been slow in coming there. For example, secondary-school education for girls in Saudi Arabia began only in the mid-1950s, whereas in Egypt it was 1925; and university education started in the 1960s, whereas in Egypt it was 1929.[12]

Yusuf Idris, who came to be regarded as the leading short-story writer in Egypt and throughout the Arab world, offers the following impressions with regard to women writers in Arabia:

> Over the last few years, collections of short stories have started reaching me from Arabia and the Persian Gulf States. It is true that most of them are by male writers, but a good number are by female writers. This is really amazing: the Arab woman in Arabia and the Persian Gulf States is almost isolated from public life. Many women there work as physicians, teachers, and bank employees (there are special banks for women), but their existence as an independent entity, and as a political or

Introduction

social force, is almost completely on the periphery of public life.

Yet the Arab woman there is a live being, cultured, well-informed, and moved by all the desires and ambitions that move the human soul. However, her wishes and ambitions have a very low ceiling which she is not allowed to pass through. Because of this, she channels her interest into writing. She finds an outlet in it, and speaks through it. Her writing may take the form either of poetry or of prose, but the short story takes up the largest share.

One day not very long ago I was busy studying these collections of feminist stories. Studying not like a casual reader, but like an investigator who knows, or claims to know, the oppressive force which brings the word out from the depths of the soul and onto the paper.

And after I had finished reading a number of collections, I discovered that I was not reading short stories in the accepted sense of the word "story," nor even in the modern sense; I was reading something different, or a different kind of writing, which was not a story and not a poem, not a tale and not scattered thoughts. A new and strange kind of writing which the Arab woman who lies far away from the course of events has invented in order to *do* with it something that will confirm to her that she is a live being, indeed a person who possesses the power of reaction and action. A writing action, which comes out under feverish pressure; and this overpowering feverish pressure interferes in the writing's formation to the extent that it appears like a puzzle to the reader. She wants to say something and yet she does not want to say it. She wants to express something and at the same time she does not want anyone to grasp her expression—I might almost say *her secret*.

And thus I found myself giving a name to this kind of

An Arabian Mosaic

writing by female writers from Arabia and the Persian Gulf States: "the short story from behind a veil."[13]

Yusuf Idris proceeds to illustrate his concluding remark with the story "From Shahrazad's Nights" by the Saudi writer Ruqayya al-Shabeeb. Written in a surrealistic style, this particular narrative draws heavily on the Arab cultural heritage and plays on multiple associations and connotations in the reader's mind. In the present work there are three representatives from Arabia: Layla al-Uthman (Kuwait), Khayriyya al-Saqqaf (Saudi Arabia), and Sharifa al-Shamlan (Saudi Arabia).

Egypt, which has always been in the forefront of literary and cultural activity in the Arab world and which offers women a greater degree of freedom compared with other Arab countries, has, as a result, a greater representation of women writers on the literary scene. Gathered in this anthology are Alifa Rifaat, Ihsan Kamal, Nawal al-Saadawi, Latifa al-Zayat, Sufi Abdallah, and Sakina Fuad. Interestingly, although Arab women writers may be geographically distanced miles away from one another, their work, whether consciously or unconsciously, often exhibits striking similarities. Nawal al-Saadawi (Egyptian, b. 1930), Latifa al-Zayat (Egyptian, b. 1925), and Layla al-Uthman (Kuwaiti, b. 1945) have each written a short story entitled "The Picture" ("al-Sura"). Not only are these stories structured around the same object—a picture—but they also have the same subject—female sexuality. However, each story deals with a different phase in a woman's life: in Nawal al-Saadawi's "Picture" it is adolescence, in Latifa al-Zayat's it is adulthood, and in Layla al-Uthman's it is middle age.

Introduction

Thus, taken together, the stories provide a unique articulation of the female experience over a complete life cycle. The connecting thread between the individual presentation of one particular phase and another is that each instance features a traumatic experience that captures a specific moment of truth, and this moment of truth brings a flash of recognition and the acquisition of indelible awareness.

"Suffering is the sole origin of consciousness" wrote Dostoyevsky: in Nawal al-Saadawi's story the budding little girl comes upon her much-admired father raping the maid in the kitchen; in Latifa al-Zayat's story the vulnerable young wife is publicly confronted with her husband's infidelity; and in Layla al-Uthman's story the insecure middle-aged woman looking for reassurance in an extramarital love affair stumbles upon an image of her own confused self in another woman. Each built around a photograph or a portrait, all three stories reiterate the thought that "true vision is always twofold: it involves emotional comprehension as well as physical perception."[14]

Stylistically, the fiction of the Arab women writers gathered here displays a variety of modes. It includes straightforward realistic description (Samira Azzam, Alifa Rifaat), poetic portrayal (Kulit Suhayl al-Khuri), symbolic depiction of characters and events (Sakina Fuad, Layla Bin Mami), surrealistic presentation (Khayriyya al-Saqqaf), and montage (Sharifa al-Shamlan). Whatever the style, these women writers demonstrate that they are responding creatively and individually to their human condition. They interpret their feminine experiences intuitively and offer a forceful account of the reality of their lives, of social psychology, and of social interaction. The resonance of their literary rhythms transcends the dominant male fabric of their culture and reiterates an aspiration to achieve recognition as valuable members of society, endowed with their own distinct talents.

Dalya Cohen-Mor

Notes

[1] Virginia Woolf, "A Room of One's Own," in Miriam Schneir (ed.), *Feminism: The Essential Historical Writings* (New York, Vintage Books, 1972), p. 345.
[2] Ibid., p. 350–51.
[3] For transcripts of the trial, see Elizabeth Warnock Fernea and Basima Qattan Bezirgan (eds.), *Middle Eastern Muslim Women Speak* (Austin, Texas, University of Texas Press, 1988), pp. 280–90.
[4] Yusuf al-Sharuni, *The 1002nd Night* (*al-Layla al-Thaniya ba'da al-Alf*, Cairo, 1975), pp. 10–11. Translation mine.
[5] Fatima Mernissi, *Doing Daily Battle*, trans. Mary Jo Lakeland (New Jersey, Rutgers University Press, 1989), p. 13.
[6] Ibid., p. 14.
[7] Ibid.
[8] Ibid.
[9] Evelyne Accad and Rose Ghurayyib (eds.), *Contemporary Arab Women Writers and Poets* (monograph series of the Institute for Women's Studies in the Arab World, Beirut University College, 5, 1985), p. 10.
[10] Evelyne Accad, *Veil of Shame* (Sherbrooke, Quebec, Editions Naaman, 1978), pp. 14–15.
[11] Ibid., pp. 32–59, 60–92.
[12] Margot Badran and Miriam Cooke (eds.), *Opening the Gates: A Century of Arab Feminist Writing* (Bloomington, Indiana, Indiana University Press, 1990), p. xxiii.
[13] Yusuf Idris, "Yusuf Idris Presents a New Female Writer" ("Yu-

suf Idris Yuqaddimu Katiba Jadida''), *al-Shumou* (a monthly magazine for arts and literature, published in Nicosia), 3 (May 1986), pp. 86–87. Translation mine.

[14] Rose Parmenter.

The Breeze of Youth
ULFA AL-IDILBI

THE GRANDMOTHER SAW HER GRANDDAUGHTER ARranging her hair in front of the mirror and said:
"Where are you going? To the university or to a wedding? Since when do schoolgirls do their hair and put on makeup? Everything's so different nowadays. How much tighter are you going to make your clothes? Have you no fear of God? You, schoolgirls! Your troubles affect us all! God has kept the rain from us, so prices have gone up again, and He's inflicted locusts, and epidemics, and foreigners on us, and removed compassion from people's hearts. All of that because of you, and you haven't learned your lesson! But you're not the only one to blame. Your father's guilty as well. He doesn't listen to me, he doesn't put his foot down and make you behave. Yesterday's men and today's are worlds apart! When I was your age, my father once saw me making myself pretty in front of the mirror—and I was already a widow and the mother of a child. He took me by the hair, slapped me hard, and said to me in a tone so harsh I still remember it: 'Who are you making yourself pretty for, you wicked girl? I won't have daughters who spend hours in front of the mirror! Understand?' Since that day, I've never had my hair done or put powder on my face. God have mercy on him! He

An Arabian Mosaic

knew how to raise daughters . . . As for your father, he'll regret it when regret will be no use. Whoever said 'The worry over girls lasts from birth till death' was right.''

But the girl, who was already eighteen, did not pay any attention to her grandmother's chatter. She continued, unhurriedly, to dress up in front of the mirror. Then she put her books under her arm and bounded down the stairs, three at a time, humming a popular song.

When she got out onto the street, she saw a group of her classmates. She exchanged greetings with them, then joined the group, blending in. She walked with a spring in her step, the wind playing with the thick tresses of hair that hung down around her shoulders. Meanwhile, her grandmother stood on the balcony and watched her from a distance, anger and envy simmering in her heart and burning in her eyes. She was contrasting her own life, lived under the burden of traditions and restrictions, with the free, unfettered life, enjoyed by the girls of the new generation. Suddenly she said to herself:

"What are we compared with today's girls?! What have we seen of this world? May God never forgive you, Father, and never be kind to you. You nipped my youth in the bud. You deprived me of everything, even the pleasures of reading and writing, which many of the girls of my generation enjoyed. By God, I don't understand. What benefit did you derive from all this?''

Then she pulled over a chair, sat down on it, and began to reflect. The sight of her granddaughter, of that ebullient youthfulness, stirred faraway memories in her. The days of her childhood and youth began to pass in her mind . . . Are the memories of childhood and youth not like the moist breezes that pass over a dead land, suddenly turning its dry stalks green and transforming its thorns into roses and lilies?

But for her, there was only one such moist breeze. As she sat there, the memory flashed through her mind, and suddenly she was fourteen again, wearing a white, shapeless gown, and such a thick veil over her face that she could hardly see through it. Escorted by her mother to buy new shoes, she was stumbling along the narrow alleys of Damascus. They arrived at the Hamadiyya bazaar and went into a shoe shop. A young salesman, who appeared to be the shop-owner's son, received them and skillfully began to display his merchandise, enumerating its qualities. A pair of black patent shoes took her fancy.

She sat on a chair to try them on. The salesman leaned down in front of her to help her put them on; her mother, meanwhile, was busy selecting another pair for herself. Suddenly the young salesman ran his hand over her leg, then held her foot between his hands and squeezed it a little. He then whispered sweetly: "Praise be to the Creator! I have seen many things in this shop, but never before have I come across such tiny, delicate feet!"

His daring touch sent a shudder through her body. She was excited and confused. Then she pulled her legs away from him and dropped the hem of her dress. He lifted his head and stared at her with a sweet, enticing smile. But how could he see anything through her thick black veil?!

She, on the other hand, could see every bit of him. A round, dark-skinned face, thick black eyebrows, and shining eyes. It was as if their shine had bored through the veil and settled on her eyes. She had to lower them and mutter, "May God preserve him for his mother."

An Arabian Mosaic

When she left, carrying her new shoes under her arm, he followed her with a look that devoured her completely. She began to walk proud and upright at her mother's side. Until that moment, she had been completely unaware that she possessed beauty capable of provoking the praises of the Creator.

Hardly had she moved away from the shop when a young man with features just like those of the shoe salesman came toward her. All of a sudden, her hand stretched unconsciously down and lifted the hem of her gown, as if she were afraid it would get dirty from the filth on the street. Her well-shaped legs appeared.

But the stupid youth didn't see what had been exposed for him! Instead, an ugly old man with a big nose and protruding eyeballs saw her legs. He screamed at her in a hoarse voice exactly like her father's: "Drop your gown, girl. May God oppress the life of girls and turn every hundred of them into one."

She felt as if a bucket of hot water had been poured on her. She dropped her gown and walked, shrunken, behind her mother till they reached their home.

It was the twenty-seventh day of the month of Rajab.[1] When the time arrived between the sunset prayer and the evening prayer, her father sat in the middle of the large sitting room and all the family gathered in a circle around him. In a humble voice he started to recite to them the story of the Mi'raj.[2] Soon, he got to the passage that says: "When the prophet, peace be on him, was in the Fifth Heaven, he asked to see Hell. Among the things he

---

[1] The seventh month of the Islamic calendar.
[2] The miraculous ascension of the prophet Muhammad from Jerusalem to the Seven Heavens.

The Breeze of Youth

saw there were women hanging by their hair. He asked, 'Oh my brother Gabriel, what is the matter with those women who are hanging by their hair?' And the angel answered, 'Those are women who showed their attractiveness to men.' "

At that moment it seemed to her that her father was casting a penetrating glance in her direction. Her heart began to beat violently, and she remembered how the young salesman had flirted with her, how she had behaved toward the youth, and how the old man had rebuked her. The image of the women hanging by their hair appeared in her mind, and she was seized by an overwhelming fear. In her heart, she repeatedly asked God for forgiveness. She performed the evening prayer, then retired early to deliberate the matter. The deliberation ended with the conclusion that she had not at all intended to entice, God knows. The young salesman had praised the Creator for the uniqueness of His creation when he had seen her legs. Was it wrong, she wondered, for the servants of God to praise the Almighty God, the Maker of slender legs and tiny, delicate feet?

On this basis, which seemed very logical to her, and in spite of her shapeless gown and thick black veil, she began to allow herself to resort to diverse tricks to show her attractiveness and beauty whenever she passed by dark-skinned youths with shining eyes.

Two weeks passed, then one morning her mother surprised her with a question: "What's the matter with you? You're so somber looking and distracted. You spend so much time on your own, and you're eating and sleeping very little."

She became confused and made a flimsy excuse to her

An Arabian Mosaic

mother to divert her attention from what was going on inside her. Deep in her heart she wished she could admit the truth to her. But what could she tell her? About the intense yearning for the dark-skinned face and the shining eyes? Or about the persistent desire for the daring touch and the sweet whispers? Oh, how she longed to see her admirer, the shoe salesman, once more. The passion of love tormented her till she could bear it no longer. His handsome image appeared in her mind day and night, and his sweet whispers rang in her ears continuously. Some nights his apparition accompanied her till morning.

But there was no way to see him again, not before those damned shoes were worn out. She took the shoes and examined them closely. They were very strong; it could take a whole year to wear them out!

A whole year?! What an eternity! She would never be able to endure it.

She thought a little and suddenly her face lit up. She hurried back to her mother, and with an air of dismay she said: "Mother! My little brother took one of my new shoes to the park and threw it into the canal. The water swept it away!" She began to sob. The mother went to her wrongly accused little son, who was too young to explain himself, and punished him. Then she returned to her grief-stricken daughter and stopped her tears by promising that they would go the next day to the same shoe salesman. Perhaps he would agree to make one new shoe; if not, they would buy a whole new pair.

When they were on their way to him, she was filled with sweet aspirations and pleasant dreams. She said to herself: "Last time he praised God. But this time I will provoke him to say the words 'There is no god but God' and 'God is great.' "

But when they entered the shop, he was not there; he had gone away on business, and his father had taken his place. For the first time in her life, she realized she was ill-fated.

Oh yes, she was ill-fated, there was no doubt about that. On the evening of that very day, her father received from the ugly old man with the big nose and the protruding eyeballs a bag containing one hundred gold pounds: it was payment for his daughter's hand. The old man had been taken with her beauty when he had met her by chance on the street and rebuked her for raising the hem of her gown. He had followed her to find out where she lived, and on that ill-omened night he had come to ask for her hand, because he desired her. Her father welcomed him and gave him his word, but he refused to let the old man go until the money had been paid.

That day marked her last contact with love and the beloved!

These pictures from the remote past sprang up one after the other in the old woman's mind. When they had reached their sorry conclusion, her eyes filled with tears and she heaved a deep and fervent sigh for her lost youth and long life, which now seemed drab and worthless to her. She choked with grief. She shook her head a number of times and looked into the distance with a wandering glance, as if she were reading the long book of her life. On the opposite balcony, she noticed the figure of an attractive young girl. She wiped her glasses, put them back on, and peered hard at the figure. "Goodness me!" she said. "That's our neighbor, Umm Anton. . . . By

An Arabian Mosaic

God, I thought she was a twenty-year-old girl! If it hadn't been for her purple shawl, I wouldn't have recognized her. Umm Anton is much older than I am, but she still wears makeup. All the women do that—except me! Why don't I try it—even if it's just once?!"

Hardly had the thought occurred to her when she hurried to her granddaughter's room and started fiddling with the little drawers that contained the granddaughter's cosmetics. She finally managed to open them, and what she saw dazzled her: boxes and bottles of different kinds and sizes, objects made of thin, shining metal with ivory handles, and pretty lipsticks in different shades of red— some light, some dark, others with a yellowish or bluish tinge. There was also a scissor-handled instrument with an end like half a circle. She had once seen her granddaughter do her eyelashes with it and had mockingly said: "I hope you stab your eyeballs with it, and die for the sake of beauty."

No, that instrument was very dangerous. She would never use it. Nothing she inspected appealed to her, except a bottle containing a sticky white liquid. She turned it upside down in her hand, then said to herself: "This must be the solution the hairdresser applied to my face on my wedding night. It really has a magical effect . . ." She began to paint her face with it. Then she looked searchingly at the mirror and said: "By God, I'm much prettier than Umm Anton!"

She then picked up a small bottle containing a shiny red liquid. She was taken with its shine. When she opened it, a sharp smell drifted to her nose, but she took some of the liquid from the bottle anyway and applied it to her cheeks and lips. Suddenly, an ugly face was looking at her from the mirror. Its ugliness startled her and she began to move backward, step by step. Unmindful of her surroundings, she stumbled against a marble statue that her granddaughter had placed near the mirror and fell to the floor. The statue fell on top of her, hitting her head, and she lost consciousness.

The following morning at the riding club, her eighteen-year-old granddaughter was puffing away on an expensive cigarette and saying to her friends:

"I don't know what happened to my poor grandmother yesterday. When I left her in the morning, she was fine, giving me her usual lecture. But when I came back from the university, I discovered she had gone into my room while I was away—which is unlike her—and had broken a statue, *Venus, the twentieth century,* which an artist friend had sculpted to look just like me. It's a shame. It was a wonderful piece . . . She had fiddled with my drawers and left them all untidy. She had covered her face with a whole bottle of expensive hair oil, and she had painted her cheeks with nail polish. Her face is so wrinkled it was impossible to get it off. And all the time she was raving about a dark-skinned young man with thick eyebrows and shining eyes. Whenever she saw me, she uncovered her old legs and asked me, quite seriously, 'Have you ever seen anything more beautiful than these?' And then again, 'Don't you think I'm prettier than Umm Anton?'"

One boy with a malicious sense of humor remarked: "Who knows? Perhaps a moist breeze from your grandmother's youth blew over her yesterday and affected her mind!"

This prompted a peal of laughter from the girls and a guffaw amongst the boys.

A Mistake in the Knitting
IHSAN KAMAL

I HAD TOLD HER REPEATEDLY THAT I DIDN'T LIKE knitting. It required a lot of patience, which I didn't have, to make a complete garment stitch by stitch. Then she would philosophize and say, "A journey of a thousand miles begins with one step." I also reminded her that since childhood I had been terrible at knitting and excellent at sewing. How nice sewing was! The material was there from the start, and all I had to do to turn it into a complete dress was to sew up the sides and shoulders. But my sister insisted, saying it was now almost a tradition one had to follow: every girl must give her fiancé a sweater she had knitted herself.

"What about a ready-made one?" I asked. "What's wrong with that?"

"He'll feel your affection for him more if you knit it yourself. Also, a ready-made one won't fit him," she answered.

"Then do me a good turn and make it for him yourself. Knitting's easy for you. Think how often you've presented us with your masterpieces!"

"Suzanne, my darling," she said. "Are you really stupid or do you just pretend to be? The woman who first thought of this didn't do it for nothing. When you decide to knit a sweater for your fiancé, making a front and back and two sleeves out of nothing, you'll naturally think of him while you're working, stitch by stitch, and with every stitch he'll get closer to your soul, and his love will steal into your heart."

She was right. As I knitted, I thought of him. But with every stitch, I cursed the day I had met him. When some friends and I heard about the way my mother had got married—which, I discovered, was the same way all their mothers had got married—I felt sorry for her and them. It was not a marriage but a gamble, even though my mother tried to play it down by calling it "an unopened watermelon." Why shouldn't it be "an opened watermelon"?[1] But even we—the few girls who are university educated and claim to be liberated and sophisticated—cut with a knife that reveals only a little bit. We may discover the color, for example, whereas taste, smell, and hardness will remain a secret in the heart of the watermelon. After all, what person reveals all his character to his friends? Even after our engagement, I went out with him for a whole month before I discovered how despicable he was. Yes, he was despicable; I could not describe it otherwise. He said he wanted details of my salary from now on, and when I expressed astonishment, he tried to appear tolerant.

"You can enjoy the months left till our wedding."

"And after that?" I pressed him further. His attitude astounded me.

"The wife's time belongs to her husband and her

---

[1] This refers to the way in which a watermelon can be bought in the Middle East: either unopened, in which case the buyer does not know if it is ripe, or cut open on the spot, in which case the buyer can refuse it if it is not ripe.

A Mistake in the Knitting

home. If she uses it to do work, the pay goes back to the original owner of the time. The owner of a car, for example, is entitled to the revenue if it's used as a taxi."

I almost felt sick. He tried to be charming, but was it really charm? I may allow a person to rob me, if he steals in soft words. "Entitled," "revenue," "owner," "time," "car," "use"—he wasn't talking, he was throwing bricks, and it wasn't the first time either. On every visit, he had brought a brick to throw at me. Perhaps I hadn't noticed them because they were small, but that day I piled them one on top of the other, and suddenly they turned into a big barrier between us.

I thought seriously about breaking the engagement, although I knew this wouldn't be a simple matter for my father and family. Their roots lay in Upper Egypt, and they clung to certain beliefs. In fact, it wasn't simple for me either. There was my reputation to consider, and the gossip. I knew that kind of gossip very well. I had heard it on previous occasions. I had even taken part in it once—among us, the educated girls. The girl in question had hardly left the room when a female colleague winked.

"She's going to meet *him*, the man who broke the engagement."

"It's unlikely. But then she has to say that."

"I wonder why he left her."

But families and neighbors aren't satisfied with assumptions, they look for certainties; they don't inquire about reasons, they're ready with speculations. Why? Is it because in the marriage game men are the strongest, and society is always in the grip of the strongest? Or do they consider man to be a treasure and find it inconceivable that a girl who's stumbled on a man would give him up? For some men this is true, but others are worth no more than a straw. Perhaps our society regards a girl as a drowning person who has to hang on even to a piece of straw. And we may indeed be drowning girls: we've left our old traditions and plunged into the sea of life, striking out for the opposite bank—liberation. But it seems we haven't reached it yet. Perhaps our daughters will manage to get there. Our generation is the generation of sacrifice. If only we hadn't left the first bank, despite its emptiness!

Well, when I insisted on not having family supervision and raised objections on the basis of my age and sophistication, I got what I wanted. We began to go out alone, without a chaperon. There was only the promise of marriage, confirmed by two rings. So that gave us quite a lot of scope. Nothing much happened, but who can prove that to people? My mother told me: "From now on every young man will hesitate a hundred times before asking for your hand."

I knew all the difficulties I would have to face even before my mother listed them for me. She looked at things through a magnifying glass. Could it be that she had convinced me? Of course not. It was inconceivable. But when he came to see me the next day, I didn't say anything. I didn't even tell him how angry his views had made me. I pretended I was sad because a movie star I adored had died. Perhaps I was afraid *he* would be the one to break the engagement. It would be a disaster. It seemed my mother had given me her magnifying glass along with her love and jewelry.

I thought I'd knitted enough: my sister had told me the

A Mistake in the Knitting

border had to be ten centimeters deep and assured me the border was the only difficult part; the rest was very easy. But what did I see? A mistake in the middle of the border! The right stitch was where the left stitch should be, and the left where the right should be. How ugly it looked, like a chessboard! But to fix it I had to undo everything above it, about six rows, every one containing more than two hundred stitches that I had strained my eyes to produce. Every time I had completed a row, I had looked at it, reassuring myself that the sweater had grown. Must I now go back and undo everything? And what would happen if his excellency wore a sweater with one mistake in it? It was inconceivable for me to start all over again: I hated knitting, just as I had started hating the sweater's intended owner. But why should I tell him that? Perhaps he had changed his character. Yes, why should I be so negative that I had to withdraw at the first setback?

The next day I went out with him, and when he headed toward the pastry shop, I firmly made him understand that I would never allow myself to be ridiculed in front of the staff there, from the manager down to the waiters, as had happened on previous occasions. He didn't buy a cake, but it was a hollow victory. All the time we sat on the terrace talking, it was clear his views remained as strange as ever.

"They're thieves! Selling a piece of cake for five piasters, when outside it costs half that amount! We'll order tea in exchange for sitting here, and that'll be enough. I'm not bothered if the waiters look at us disapprovingly or the manager objects. Let them go to hell.

An Arabian Mosaic

Those who buy people's respect by forking out more money are stupid and hypocritical.''

I'd tried every argument, but I couldn't convince him. On the other hand, *I* became convinced—convinced that this was not a positive outlook at all. Being positive means overcoming obstacles with a view to improving the future. The positive approach encourages one to crush any mountains that stand in the way of the future—as is happening now in Aswan, for example.[2] But changing a character is an impossible task. Our ancestors rightly said that character leaves the body only after the soul. How on earth did I think I could change him? Take me, for example. Although I was younger and belonged to the so-called weaker sex, could anyone change my values and turn me into a slave of materialism? Impossible! Being positive, in my personal situation, meant courageously and decisively severing the ties that bound our two lives, refusing a marriage that from the outset clearly seemed sure to fail, and choosing a route to happiness that differed totally from his way of life.

"Valentine leaves the earth's orbit and circles in space." I pushed the newspaper aside. I thought it would distract me, but it only increased my anger. I was unable to break through stupid convictions that people had acquired. People *here*, only here. Everywhere else in the world people regard an engagement as a trial period for the two partners and assume that if they break up, it means they lacked mutual understanding. But in our country—or in our conservative circle, to be precise—

---

[2] The reference is to the construction of the Aswan Dam.

A Mistake in the Knitting

my mother, for example, said the trial should *precede* the engagement. My God, Mother, how did you arrive at that?! Suppose he were my classmate, even then much of his personality—the very part that concerns the future sharer of his life—would remain hidden from me. How much more so, then, when he was not my classmate! How could he be? He had graduated from the university a year before I joined it. He was a classmate of Afaf's, my spoiled friend who had a relaxed attitude to studying, took two years to complete one year's program, and graduated with me. A few months before her graduation, she introduced me to Shukri Abd al-Aziz. He had used the opportunity provided by his transfer to Cairo to come to the department to register his master's thesis as the first step toward a doctorate. The faculty regulations allowed only those who had obtained at least a grade of "good" to register for postgraduate work, and he tried to overcome this obstacle by making frequent visits to the department.

He saw us every time he came to the department. Afaf seemed to be expecting him to ask her to marry him, but he approached me instead. Our superficial acquaintance meant I knew very little about him, and this little appealed to me—until I discovered that I had misunderstood his behavior and that the truth was quite the opposite of what I assumed. I admired his scholarly ambition in trying desperately to overcome the faculty's regulations—until he told me sarcastically that he hadn't given a thought to ambition or intellectual status, and that his only motive was the high salary the degree would bring. I also liked his unselfishness and his lack of that trait, latent in most Middle Eastern men, which pushes them to try to appear superior to their wives. That was when he started introducing me to all his friends as a doctoral candidate. I realized finally that he was motivated by vanity. I was even wrong about the way I thought he viewed me, the woman who would share his life. I believed he preferred intelligence and character to beauty, for there was no denying that Afaf was much prettier than I. In fact, I was merely a more lucrative deal, because of my expected degree. So I started to hate the degree, having originally felt so enthusiastic about it. His calculating attitude was not something I figured out after getting to know his personality: he revealed it to me by a few slips of the tongue.

How could I marry a person I didn't respect? How could I live with him day after day, year after year, when our views clashed every time we met? Married life does not consist only of the meeting of two bodies, or else we would be just like animals: it would be enough for a male, any male, to meet a female, any female. Married life is first and foremost a rapprochement of the character and mind of a man and a woman as they set out together on the long journey of life.

What about the other option? Gossip, rumors, and the conjectures of envious people. As long as I was successful in my study and work, there would be no escape from them. I had female neighbors and relatives whose scholastic scores were not high enough to get them to university, or who went there and then dropped out—to the relief of their mothers, who said: "Our daughters won't be working alongside male colleagues!" And my cheerful, outgoing companions, from whom I would maintain a reserved and dignified distance, would all talk about

A Mistake in the Knitting

"his deception," even those who didn't dislike me. Everywhere I would encounter burning question marks in the eyes of my male colleagues and scorn in the eyes of my female colleagues. No sooner would I turn my back than pairs of heads would draw together and the chitchat would begin. Our liberation has only been external. Our thoughts still wear the veil.

What would be my own position on all this? Should I rise above all the gossip and toss it aside with indifference, or should I try to clarify things to everybody?

Why does the human soul have a predilection for mocking other people's misfortune? Why did fate yesterday cause that white-suited old man with the elegant flywhisk to fall down in front of our balcony? When he got up from the muddy ground, his suit was spotted like a leopard's skin. Everybody on the street and on our balcony burst out laughing. Wouldn't it have been more appropriate for them to show sorrow? And when a wedding engagement is broken, either by the woman or the man, doesn't it imply the failure of a plan that the woman dreamed would bring her happiness? One would think, then, that she would receive commiseration, sympathy, and cooperation from those around her. But I too had an excuse for attaching importance to gossip. Regardless of how developed and civilized we have become, we are unable to ignore people's views or what they say about us, as long as we live among them. I had even read in foreign novels about people who were stricken by despair or ridden with complexes because of unfair rumors.

After that little incident at the pastry shop, the scales were balanced, although the scale for breaking the engagement was beginning to tilt downwards. So I was still hesitating when he left after visiting me yesterday evening. I didn't quite end our relationship, but I didn't go out with him either. I was like someone who has encountered some danger on the road in front of him, but who knows the road behind him is not clear either, and who chooses to stand still, in the middle of the road. Yet nothing in the world can stand still like that. Even the knitting in my hands was growing.

If that piece of wool had become so dear to me, then it's no wonder psychologists ascribe a mother's love for her children to her efforts in carrying and bearing them, and then in serving and caring for them. I looked at the knitting fondly. It had come into existence through a lot of effort involving the collaboration of my hands and eyes. It was also a big secret. He hadn't seen the sweater in my hands until yesterday. Before that I had attempted to hide it, wanting it to be a surprise. I no longer cared. Of course he had to express his joy.

"You're making it yourself? That's wonderful! You can't imagine how much cheaper it is than the ready-made ones!"

In spite of his "encouragement," I was still working on the sweater this morning. Alone. I no longer felt bored, sitting by myself. I worked in complete silence and a deep serenity that were hardly disturbed by the friction of the needles or the movement of the ball of wool. When I pulled the thread, the ball jumped around, like a happy, lively bird. The needles worked by themselves, or so it sometimes seemed to me. Like two magician's batons, their touch changed the loose thread into a solid weave. In my mind they resembled a writer's pen, creating a story from separate words, or a compos-

A Mistake in the Knitting

er's quill, combining scattered tunes into a symphony. The needles embraced each other, then disengaged, only to embrace again. They could not be separated. The woollen weave united them like an inescapable destiny. And they were content with their interconnected destiny. I heard no violent clash when they met, only a soft rustling, like a light kiss. The bird on the thread continued to dance in spite of the approaching end. It was as if it were happy to give its blood, drop by drop, so that a love story or symphony could be written. How far I still was from all that—at the other end of the world! He was delighted about the sweater and showed a lot of appreciation for my having made it, just as you predicted, sister. But you meant one thing, and he meant another . . . I wished my sister would come to see us, so that I could argue it out with her in front of the Lord in heaven. She had made me struggle for nothing . . . Talk of the devil!

She came along, cheerful and carefree. "Amazing!" she exclaimed. "You've almost finished the front."

"Yes. Yesterday I decreased the stitches for the arms, and now I'm starting to decrease for the collar."

I laid it down in front of her, and she looked at it closely, delighted. Suddenly she let out a great groan of dismay.

"There's a mistake in the middle of the border," she said mournfully.

"Yes," I answered with indifference. "I only noticed it after several rows."

"You have to undo everything until you get there," she said, and acted on her words. She drew out the needles, then pulled the thread. Her action so startled me that for a while I just looked at her, taken aback,

An Arabian Mosaic

unable to speak or move. Finally I awoke from my amazement, rushed at the sweater, and tried to snatch it from her.

"No, no," I screamed. "You can't do that! I worked so hard on it and put so much effort into it. I slaved day after day, night after night. You can't destroy all that in one second."

"It's your fault!! You should have gone back to the row with the mistake in it as soon as you discovered it—while you were still at the beginning—so you could do it again correctly. How can you build anything on faulty foundations? Once you discovered the serious flaw, you should never have gone on. Never!"

My Wedding Night
Alifa Rifaat

THE DREAM OF MY YOUTH WAS THE DREAM OF EVERY virgin whose body youth had touched with magic and exhilarated, turning it into a luscious figure intoxicated with desire . . . and whose songs revolved around the moment when she would give herself and all her delights to her chosen man on her wedding night.

And here was my wedding night. It arrived to find me sad, my spirit broken, my wings cut off, my heart moaning in fear and beating in confusion. In front of me a dancer was swaying, moving slowly on the floor to the rhythm of the loud music and the beating of the reverberating drums. She clashed her cymbals, and all the guests became enraptured and swayed with her, happy. I was the only one annoyed by her shameless nakedness and the dissolute story she was telling, her belly trembling till the tremor of ecstasy seized those surrounding her, and they began to clap their hands in excitement. I was the only one who was feeling upset, so upset that I was twisted in pain and had difficulty breathing. Perhaps the fear that gripped me had sparked my imagination.

Roses surrounded me, forming a large bouquet around my seat and the seat of the man to whom I was being given. But this throne over which I presided seemed to me nothing but a bier packed with frozen roses. Suddenly it would tumble with me into a bottomless grave, dark, like the obscure future that I faced. I was suffocating. I was suffocating. I wanted to rise up amid the people crowded around me. I wanted to run away. I didn't think anyone shared my suffering, or paid any attention to it. I couldn't understand why they didn't take pity on me and go away. What was the benefit, anyway, of inviting them to my wedding night? I felt shy and confused at the thought that they all knew what would happen to me. I was so frightened and so overwhelmed by this sensation that I was no longer able to move or rise. I didn't feel time passing; it passed as I played the heroine in this ongoing comedy they called the wedding celebration. Why should I rejoice when I was about to take on a heavy responsibility and a lot of hard work? Everybody had been preparing for this celebration for days, right up to the promised night. The house, decorated with lights and flowers, was filled with people. Large quantities of drink were being poured, piles of splendid sweets were being served. But I felt that this house, my father's house, where I grew up, had become strange to me. The moment I signed the marriage contract, I became a guest in it; nothing there concerned me. Grief squeezed my heart at the thought that I would be leaving it in a few moments. "Why, then," you might ask, "did you agree to the marriage, if you harbored all this rejection in your heart?"

Well, the reason, simply, was that I was obeying my father; and our family circumstances were such that I was duty-bound to agree to this marriage. I knew full well that my father wanted to lighten the heavy burden he had been laboring under all these years. And I was

My Wedding Night

the eldest in a long line of daughters; it was my duty to clear the way for the younger ones, as our traditions decree. Also, I wanted to make my poor, sick mother happy; she had put up for years with a hard life for our sake. It makes mothers happy to see their daughters married, despite the difficulties and problems marriage brings their daughters later on.

In fact, I didn't have any great hopes about the man who, that night, had become my husband and master, a man suitable for me, as my father assured me when he congratulated me, having given his approval after an elaborate investigation of the man's personal details and affairs. My father discovered that he was a hard-working engineer from a middle-class family like ours. His father was a devout, honest man, and his mother a respectable, good woman. Together they had brought him up to be moral and principled. After graduation he worked for the government, but then a voice urged him to visit the holy places. He obeyed the call and went off, leaving behind all the temptations of life, searching for the light, trying to get near to God. His journey lasted a long time. He forgot himself, living a life of asceticism and abstinence in a humble tent on top of a mountain.

But youth was obviously still stirring in his young body, because it woke him out of his delusion, and he realized that true faith meant struggling and being ready to grapple with the temptations of the devil; it didn't mean deprivation, introversion, and confinement. So he went back to his family and looked for a wife.

His mother, who was a friend of my mother, asked for my hand on his behalf. I consented, content with my lot. After all, I wasn't expecting to find anyone: my sweetheart had died and left me when we were still children. We were children, but we had known true love, in all its sincerity and devotion.

    We used to hide our best candy and our best toys in order to surprise and impress each other. We would enjoy them together in complete innocence. We often stood in the garden, looking at the flowers dotted around the little fountain, and wandered about, chasing the butterflies and hornets that flew over the treetops and through the branches in blossom. Our hands were linked, and our hearts beat in union to a tune that sang of unspoiled joy at the radiance of nature.

    Our souls quietly filled with deep gratitude toward the Creator of the universe, for having filled magical cups of beauty on which we drew without ever drinking our fill. We would stand side by side, humble and entranced, as if praying to the Great Creator. Then our emotions would overflow and we would embrace, quite openly, not caring that someone might see us.

    We never thought that embracing might be forbidden. We would stretch out on the grass in each other's arms, rolling over on the carpet of dew and trying not to let go of each other. We would track little insects to their nests. Eventually we would tire of playing, and then we would lie in each other's arms, panting with exhaustion, and tenderness would flow between us, gently, serenely. Sometimes when we were together I would feel a warm, pleasant shudder, like the shudder the dancer was now trying to send through people's bodies. I would forget myself and cover my sweetheart's face with kisses, unaware of my true feelings. Our families saw us and understood; they were unable to separate us because of

My Wedding Night

the strength of our love and our determination. As they were both watching us with a smile, his mother—our neighbor—promised my mother that I would be his bride when we grew up. We were overjoyed and laughed, and the laughter came from the bottom of our hearts. He whispered, "You're my bride from now on," and I pulled him by the hand and shouted delightedly, "Come on, let's play the marriage game with our sisters."

I grabbed my mother's veil and gown, which she kept folded in the prayer rug, and draped them over my little body. That was after I had smudged my face with her crimson lipstick, turning it into a small red rose with chaotic petals . . .

The sister who succeeded me in the long line of daughters that my parents had enthusiastically borne and jealously guarded stood banging the copper coffee tray and singing the song of the wedding procession.

My other sisters swayed happily to her singing, repeating the song in their soft voices: "Walk gracefully, oh beautiful girl, oh pretty one, oh rose from the garden . . ." And I strutted along proudly and offered myself to him like a real rose that blossoms in a garden. I moved majestically, though stumbling a little on the hem of my long gown. My hand lay in my sweetheart's hand; my eyes were fastened in delight on his eyes, shining with happiness and joy. And so my heart throbbed ecstatically, and I couldn't help but join in the singing, my loud voice eventually rising above the voices of the other singers. Then my sister came to a halt and stopped banging on the tray; the procession paused, and its orderly formation disintegrated. She then rebuked me, shouting: "Don't sing. The bride's not allowed to sing."

An Arabian Mosaic

My joy suddenly dried up, and a mysterious sadness seized me. I kept asking: "Why can't I sing happily like them? Why can't the bride be happy?"

And here I was now, a real bride, and this was my wedding night. But I wasn't singing for joy, and I didn't share people's joy for me. Inside me was a heart torn apart and shaking with fear. A mysterious voice penetrated to the depths of my broken soul, urging me to refuse everything fate had brought on me and begging the angel of death to rescue me from my unknown destiny.

The shrieks of joy suddenly became louder. The drums beat quicker, the dancer whirled faster. I was astounded at her ability to create happiness and to keep smiling all this time. Everybody stood up. The knight of my night stood up too and stretched out his hand to help me to my feet. My mother, feeling shy like me, signaled to me to obey him. I stood up, my heart falling to my silver shoes, and walked, led by candles dancing in the girls' hands.

A little girl stepped on the edge of the long veil that was fastened to my hair with flowers. I almost twisted my neck. She burst out laughing, thinking of the night—*her night*—when she would be in my place. I walked, was driven, then walked again, until I found myself in a closed room with the man who had become my husband, he and I, all alone.

I stood still, bewildered, my eyes lowered in anxiety. Having sat for so long so rigidly, I didn't know how I should behave. He too stood still, confused and baffled. Then he went over to a table crammed with food and sweets. Men never forget their stomachs, no matter what the circumstances are. Or perhaps his flight to the table

My Wedding Night

was a way of relieving our embarrassing situation. We had met many times before tonight. We had gone for walks together during our engagement and talked about various subjects; but this was the first time we were meeting as man and woman, with the family all waiting for the encounter. He took a handful of food, put it in his mouth, then said in a hoarse, trembling voice: "Hungry?"

"No." My head was still lowered, and now and again I would steal a glance at him.

"You must eat something. It's going to be a long night," he insisted.

I shuddered, feeling isolated and lonely. I wished I could run to my father's arms and be rocked till I calmed down. I stumbled hurriedly behind the screen and took off the veil that was weighing down my head. I removed my white wedding gown and folded it carefully, so my mother could keep it for my sisters after me. My father had paid a huge sum for it. Then I put on the white embroidered gown prepared especially for my wedding night.

I crept into the bed, hoping to sleep and so escape the long night that hung like a threat over me. He finished eating, turned toward me, and whispered from a distance, "Kiss me." I turned my face away, anger at the ready, waiting to see what he would do.

When he reacted distantly, like a stranger, I mumbled an anxious "Good night." He turned off the light, lifted the cover, and pulled me toward him. Fear gripped me, and I began to shake. As I closed my eyes in surrender, I remembered the story of Ishmael, peace be on him, when he gave himself as a sacrifice to please his Lord and was tied to the stone by Abraham, God's friend.[1] He took off my underwear. Up to then this had been one of my intimate secrets. Just the fact of my father seeing it by accident hanging in the bathroom to dry was enough to embarrass me. My blood flowed hot, thumping in my head and making me dizzy.

He became absorbed in a long series of attempts, and I suppressed my pain and fear, waiting, expecting him to remove the barrier between us. But the nightmare dragged on endlessly. Suddenly he let go of my legs, hurried over to the light, and turned it on. I opened my eyes startled, and looked around, half expecting to see the sacrificial ram, brought down from heaven by the angel. What I did see was a man standing in the middle of the room, naked. His shapely body aroused me, but he was crying and tearing at his hair.

"The bastards did this to me."

At first I didn't understand what had happened. But I dried my martyr's tears and said fervent thanks in my heart for having been saved by the hand of God. Then the truth dawned on me: my own life was the sacrificial ram, and I had to guide my naive, innocent man, and make him play his proper role. Like me, he was a virgin; no female body had ever been near him before, just as a man's hand had never touched me before. I got up, straightened my clothes, and pulled him to me, enveloping him with tenderness and covering him with the silk bedspread, so that I could talk to him without feeling

---

[1] According to Muslim tradition, it was Ishmael, not Isaac, who was ordered to be sacrificed to God. When Abraham complied and proved his true faith, a sacrificial ram was sent down from heaven to take the place of Ishmael.

My Wedding Night

embarrassed. He calmed down a little and buried his head in my chest. Sobbing desperately, he said: "My uncle's wife did this to me because she wanted me to marry her daughter Samiyya, but my mother chose you for me because you're gentle and pure."

Consoling him, I said: "What you're worrying about doesn't bother me. Let's live together like friends, with love and compassion. They are a thousand times better than what you intended."

Beating his chest with his hands, he said in despair: "But how shall we become husband and wife?"

I answered tenderly: "I'll tell you frankly. When I was a child, I had a little sweetheart. We used to hug each other, quite innocently, and he would lay his head on my chest, and we would lie there for hours, cozy and peaceful. Why don't we do that now, till we fall sleep?"

"You think that fulfills the marriage contract?" he asked angrily.

"Can you manage anything else at the moment?" I answered teasingly.

My nonchalance had infected him, and he said: "Certainly not! I'm tired."

"Then let's hold each other, and try to get in tune with each other, and just let things develop with time," I said cheerfully.

"Will I be able to, one night?" he asked hopefully.

"Love works miracles," I answered ecstatically, as my anxiety vanished.

"Come on, then. We'll start our life together as children," he said, happy.

As he took me in his arms gently and affectionately, I

laughed knowingly and said: "I think we're going to grow up fast tonight."

We lay in each other's arms on the bed, exchanging kisses and ignoring that persistent flicker. Then we turned off the light—he was calm again—and surrendered to the hoped-for dream. As you know, it was my wedding night . . .

Tears for Sale
Samira Azzam

I do not know how it was possible for Khazna to be a mourner for the dead and a hairdresser for brides at the same time. I had heard a lot about her from my mother and her friends before I had the opportunity to see her for the first time—when one of our neighbors died. Not yet fifty, this man was already consumed by disease, and so it came as no surprise when one of our female neighbors said to my mother, without sadness: "He's dead, Umm Hasan. May evil never befall us."

I got the feeling I was about to experience a colorful day full of excitements, and it pleased me. I could take advantage of being a neighbor of the deceased man's family and sneak inside with the other boys and girls of the quarter to stare at the dead man's waxen face, to watch his wife and daughters weep for him, and see the female mourners rhythmically clapping their hands and chanting phrases they had learned by heart.

I took one of my little girlfriends by the hand and together we managed to sneak through the assembled men and find a place not far from the door, where lots of other children had gathered, keen, like us, to get acquainted with death and experience a few adventures. There we stayed—until a big hand pushed us aside. It was the hand of Khazna, standing, tall and broad, in the doorway. She quickly assumed a distressed look, stretched out her fingers, and undid her two braids. Then she took a black headcloth out of her pocket and tied it around her forehead. Next she gave a horrendous scream, which filled my little heart with dread, and forced her way through the women to a corner in which stood a vessel containing liquid indigo. She rubbed her face and hands with it, making herself look like the masks that vendors hang up in their shops during festivals. Then she came back and stood by the dead man's head, gave another scream, and began to beat her breast violently and roll her tongue, uttering rhythmical words which the women repeated after her. Tears were already flowing from their eyes. It was as if with her screams Khazna was mourning not only this dead man, but all the dead of the village, one by one, stirring in this woman grief over a departed husband, in that woman grief over a son or brother . . . So you could no longer tell which of the women was the mother of the deceased, or the wife, or the sister. If the women flagged in their efforts, exhausted, Khazna delivered a particularly sad eulogy, followed by a horrendous scream. And behold! The tears gushed out, the weeping increased, and the grief intensified. Khazna was the pivot in all this, with an indefatigable tongue, a voice like an owl's, and a strange ability to summon up grief. The reward was in proportion to the effort, and Khazna's recompense for her great anguish was such that it awakened in her an inexhaustible spring of grief.

I still remember how, when the men came to carry the deceased to his wooden bier, Khazna begged them to proceed gently with the dearly departed, to be careful,

Tears for Sale

and not to hasten to cut his ties with this world. This went on until one man got fed up with her chatter, pushed her away and, with the help of his friends, forcibly carried off the deceased. The black handkerchiefs were then raised in farewell, and the women's requests came flowing, this one sending greetings to a departed husband, and that one to a mother. Khazna then filled the whole place with a wailing that rang out clearly above the voices of the dozens of screaming women. Only when the funeral procession withdrew, when the bier, on which the dead man's fez was swinging, was slowly being carried away by the escorting men, did Khazna quiet down. Then it was time for the women to rest a little from the sadness that had swept over them. They were invited to help themselves to some of the food set out on a table in one of the rooms. Khazna was the first to wash her face, roll up her sleeves, and fill her big mouth with anything she could lay her hands on. As I stood among the little children who had slipped in, I noticed her hiding something in the front of her dress. Sensing she had been spotted, she gave a tired smile and said:

"It's a little something for my daughter Masuda. I got the news before I could prepare anything for her to eat. And eating the food from a mourning ceremony is counted as a good deed."

That day I understood that Khazna was different from any other woman. She was a necessity for death even more than for the dead. I would never forget her big mouth, her fearful hands, and her loose, curly hair. Whenever I heard that a man was dying, I would run with my friends to his house, prompted merely by the wish to see something exciting. I would then relate the adventure to my mother—if, that is, she had not run there herself. Then I would be distracted from the face of the dying man by the sight of Khazna, and my eyes would be glued to her, contemplating her hands as they moved from her breast to her face to her head in a violent beating which seemed, like the words she intoned, to have a special rhythm that sank into the wounds of the bereaved family and made the guests feel the grief.

Some time passed before I had the opportunity to see Khazna at a wedding. I could not believe my eyes. She had the same black curly hair, but it was combed and adorned with flowers. She also had the same ugly face, but the powders applied to it made it a far cry from the face painted with indigo. Her eyes appeared bigger because of the kohl she had used to circle them. Her arms were loaded with bracelets (who said trading in death was not profitable?), and her mouth was constantly open in laughter. She shut it only halfway to chew on a big piece of gum held between her yellow teeth.

Then I realized that Khazna had to do with brides as much as she had to do with the dead. Her task began on the morning of the wedding day. She depilated the bride with sugar syrup and penciled her eyebrows, at the same time initiating her into her sexual duties in a whisper—or what she thought was a whisper. If the bride blushed, she laughed at her and winked, reassuring her that in two or three nights she would become an expert at making love, and that she could guarantee it if the bride kept applying the fragrant soap to her body and the oil to her hair. These were things which the bride could fetch from the chemist or buy from Khazna herself. When evening came, the women flocked together, perfumed and beautifully adorned, and gathered in a circle around the bride, who sat up on a platform. Then Khazna's trills of joy tore the sky above the village asunder. She played a prominent role in the dance circle, going round joking with the women, saying obscene things which made them laugh. When, amidst the winking of the women, the bridegroom came to take the bride away, Khazna undertook to conduct them solemnly to the door of their room, where she still had the right to keep guard. I didn't quite understand why Khazna was so eager to stand at the newly-weds' door, waiting nervously and inquisitively. Whenever the signal came—after a short wait or a long one—she uttered a piercing trill of joy, which the bride's family had obviously been eagerly awaiting. When it came, the men twisted and twirled their mustaches, and all the women stood up simultaneously and uttered proud trills of joy. Then Khazna left, content in eye, soul, stomach, and pocket, the women wishing that she, in her turn, would rejoice at Masuda's wedding.

Masuda's wedding was something Khazna looked forward to. It was also the reason she collected bracelets and provisions. After all, she had no one else in the world except this daughter, and it was to her that everything she gathered up from the funerals and weddings would pass.

But the heavens did not want Khazna to rejoice.

It was a summer that I was never to forget. Typhoid ensured it was a season like no other for Khazna. The sun did not rise without a new victim, and it was said that Khazna mourned for three customers on one day.

The disease did not spare Masuda, invading her bowels, and death took no pity on her, despite Khazna's solemn pledges.

The people in my village awoke to the news of the little girl's death. Their curiosity began right where the life of this poor girl ended. How would Khazna weep for her daughter? In what manner unknown to the mourners? What kind of eulogy would her grief at the loss prompt her to deliver? And what sort of funeral ceremony would shake the people of the quarter?

Curiosity and sorrow got the better of me, and I went along to Khazna's house, together with scores of other women rushing to redeem some of their debt to her.

The house had only one room and could not contain more than twenty people. We sat down and those who could not get in remained standing in a circle at the door. I looked out over the heads, searching for Khazna's face, because I did not hear her voice. To my amazement, I didn't find her crying. She was silent, speechless, lying on the floor in the corner of the room. She had not wrapped a black brow-band round her head, or painted her face with indigo; she was not striking her cheeks or tearing at her clothes.

For the first time I saw the face of a woman who was not feigning her emotions. It was the face of a woman suffering pain, almost dying from the pain.

It was a mute grief—grief that only those who had experienced sadness or known misfortune could recognize.

Some women tried to weep or scream. But she looked at them with dismay, as if she loathed this feigning, so they fell silent, utterly amazed. When the men came to carry the body of the only creature for whom Khazna

Tears for Sale

might express her feelings without hypocrisy, she did not scream or tear at her clothes, but instead looked at them distractedly. Then she walked off behind them like someone in a daze, as they headed toward the mosque and the cemetery. All she did there was to lay her head on the earth to which the little body had been entrusted, and let it rest there for hours—God alone knows how many hours.

People came back from the funeral ceremony with different versions of what had happened to Khazna. Some said she had gone so mad that she seemed rational. Others said she had no tears left, because all those funerals had exhausted them. And there were even people who said that Khazna did not cry because she was not getting paid for it.

There were only very few people who preferred not to say anything, and leave it to Khazna—in her silence—to express it all.

The Future

Daisy al-Amir

She paid for the dress hurriedly, not even sure whether it fitted her, but aware that it was made of a thick material suitable for spring or autumn. It was now midsummer, she thought. Perhaps there really was an autumn or a spring coming, but would she see it arrive? Would there be a spring or an autumn? Last spring and autumn had not happened. Time had stood still at them, as it had stood still at all four seasons of the year. Not so the fighting, which never stood still, annihilating every minute, every whisper, every emotion, every, every, every . . . She hid the dress quickly in the bag. She didn't want to admit to herself that she was committing a crime by buying a dress while the war of destruction assailed everything. Two whole years of weeks and months? No. No. She couldn't concentrate any more. She could no longer calculate the number of weeks there were in those many months, nor the number of days, nor minutes, nor seconds. She was like everyone else, waiting every moment for news, news that was not too distressing, or news that made no mention of the massive destruction and the deep darkness.

She bought the dress at the house next to hers. She didn't have to cross a single street or go down a single flight of stairs. The lady who lived next door to her sold clothes.

The shops no longer opened for business. When she contemplated buying a dress, she felt tar would be hurled at her and her house, the sort of hot burning tar that was hurled at the houses of dishonorable women, so that every passer-by on that road would know that the house pelted with tar was inhabited by a woman afflicted by the curse of those who rebel against virtue. Then they would cut off her hair and burn her house and . . . She touched her hair with one hand, and clutched the bag that concealed the dress with the other.

The dress was for the autumn, and it was summer now. Whoever had managed to stay alive was either imprisoned in his house, or else a hero. He had been lucky—or was a coward—not to have been hit by a sniper's bullet or a rocket that had gone astray, accidentally or intentionally, or not to have been kidnapped at a roadblock, or slaughtered in the cause of religion. What other methods of dying could she recall, old and new, that people had known, or not known, over the centuries of human life?

How could she have bought a dress when minutes ago she was wondering how she could possibly get hold of bread for the next few days? If the days actually came, would the fuel she had be enough for lighting and cooking? Would there be a night when she didn't suffer hunger cramps? Had she really bought a dress, when there were hundreds and thousands of people with no roof to shelter them, and hundreds longing for a mouthful of bread, and hundreds more who were now corpses, flung about and consumed by death?!

The Future

Lebanon was dying. All the world's newspapers and news broadcasts began with reports about the fighting in Lebanon, and everybody tried to diagnose the disease, and everybody knew what it was, but there was no remedy for the chronic ailment.

Wouldn't it have been better if she had saved this money rather than buying a dress? If she had kept the money in her bag or in her cabinet, or if she had hung the dress in the wardrobe, could she be certain, she wondered, of holding on to either of them: the whole house—property, money, people—was a target for plunder. So what difference did it make whether she bought a dress or saved the money, since everything was a target for looting? The dress she had bought—where had the woman who sold it got hold of it? How did these dresses, put on display, come to be for sale? How were they bought? How were they acquired? And those who sold the dresses, did they actually buy them? Did they import them? Did they make them themselves? There were constant reports of theft from warehouses and banks and firms and private houses.

Armed people were fighting for a national cause and dying willingly as martyrs; other armed people were fighting to steal. How could you tell one from the other? Who was stealing from whom? And who was protecting the possessions of those who were not armed? Those fighting thought themselves entitled to steal and plunder places and souls. What did the armed faction in defense of the national cause do when they saw the other armed faction plundering and stealing? Was it not in the national cause *not* to let the country be plundered? Was it not in the national cause *not* to deprive the individual of his possessions, the way he was deprived of his soul?

The dress she bought was paid for with money she had earned by the sweat of her brow. So was the dress she was wearing, and there was no shame in it.

Other people . . . other people deserved to have hot burning tar hurled at them and their houses, so that every passer-by would know that true shame must be put to the flame and made public. She let her hand run over the bag containing the dress, smoothing it out. It was no longer folded up. She wanted to see someone and tell them she had bought a dress from a place whose owner sold honest goods, and that she had bought it with honest money. She wanted to scream at the top of her voice: "I didn't steal! I didn't steal! I didn't steal, and I never shall! And I'll wear the dress next spring or autumn!"

Next spring or autumn? She no longer waited for anything any more . . . She didn't know what season it was. Why think of the seasons and wait for the next minute, when in an instant the end might come . . . the end . . . death.

If she had only one moment left, wouldn't it be enough to enjoy herself and vent her anger by buying a dress with honest money from an honest shop? What did it matter whether she wore the dress or not? What mattered was that she should enjoy the moment of buying it. Save the money for the future? Was there a future? Would the morning sun rise for her?

She wanted to feel that life was going on. She wanted to feel the desire to possess. She wanted to prepare for coming days. And so, suddenly, she felt she wanted to live, to prepare for the future, for the autumn or the

The Future

spring, and have a new dress to wear. She didn't want to feel she might die at any moment. Were these excuses she was making up to get rid of feelings of guilt? Buying a new dress when people were dying from hunger, and the bombs and rockets were falling everywhere? Death was waiting for her at every corner, and she was clutching the dress, as if by clinging to it she was clinging to life.

Lebanon was dying and calling for help, while the whole world . . . the whole world, one way or another, was plunging a new knife into it, administering a new, sharp poison to it, and burying it more deeply. The world was plugging its ears with new wax, and reaching out to grab. It sent provisions that never arrived, and delegations that bartered the truth or didn't reveal it. They promised . . . acted . . . told the truth . . . lied . . .

All this was happening in Lebanon, while she . . . she was busy buying a new dress for an autumn she knew would not arrive?

The seller of the dress said that she was forced to trade at home because her husband and children had stopped working, and that she had resorted to this as a means of making a living. Even the seller had tried to justify the display of dresses for sale by the fear of hunger, whereas *she* had bought a dress for an autumn that would never come! Could the dress save her from hunger? Could it keep the sniper away from her, or the rocket, or the bomb, or the explosives? Could it possibly be an alternative to the darkness she was afraid of? Could it undo all the fearful waiting she endured in the autumn and the preceding summer? She folded the bag so that its volume would not attract attention. She folded it again, reducing its size still further. Perhaps then she would forget that she was carrying a dress in the bag, a dress just for her.

A car with fighters in it passed by. They shot into the air to frighten people, but she wasn't afraid.

She was used to the bullets and the explosives and the rockets and the darkness . . . and then again she wasn't used to any of them. She was still alive, in spite of all the dead, wounded, and mutilated people whom she saw and heard about, or whom she didn't see and didn't hear about, but . . . Did she have the right to buy a new dress on the pretext that she was still alive? And would she be able to keep it? Would her house remain safe from looting? Would she be able to get to a doctor, or would the doctor be able to get to her, if she fell ill? If she was wounded? If she got hit? Would the armed people at the roadblock give her the chance to explain that she might die if she didn't get to the hospital? And the fighters? What did the word "death" mean to them, when they had experienced death every moment and hour and day and week and month these two years? What significance did the individual have—whether he remained alive or whether the number of dead increased by tens or hundreds or thousands? When did the life of the individual ever have significance in the eyes of the fighters, who were exposed to death at every moment?

But the fighters who were exposed to death had a barricade to protect them, and weapons to defend themselves.

Weapons and fighters and commanders and leaders and chiefs and parties and followers and organizations—they approached each other and drew back, supported each other and fought each other, cursed each other and

The Future

praised each other, and she . . . she was this one individual among the thousands of other individuals who didn't belong to any of these groups. How could she protect herself from the horror of the moment, of the hour, of the day? The horror of the memories of days gone by?

Would she see the next day arrive? Would a new morning and a new sun rise after the long dark night lit by rockets? And what about *her*? So she had bought a dress for the autumn. What season was that, which they called autumn? The seller of the dress had said it was suitable for spring or autumn. Which of these seasons was nearer at hand? Which season's days would she feel and see as they really were, without having the world, and the house, and the sky shut off around her?

A bomb fell on the entrance to the building. She wasn't afraid. She didn't panic. She didn't run away. She stood motionless, observing the broken glass and listening to the cries of fear. Where did this courage come from? Was it from the future she was holding in a bag hidden under her arm? The residents of the building were hurrying to the shelter. She stood at the entrance to the staircase, watching them racing each other, screaming, their little children on their arms. She couldn't tell who was more frightened, the children or the adults. Which of them would still be alive the next minute, and which was death waiting for? And she . . . she touched the dress. Her soul was profoundly sad, unable to find a justification for buying a new dress.

The bombs came thick and fast, piercing the walls and windows. She climbed down the dark staircase, holding on to the railing, and reached the shelter door. She didn't know what made her stand motionless there, instead of rushing inside with the others.

She touched the dress and felt reassured. And yet, who could explain to her at that moment why she had bought the new autumn dress? And if anyone there saw it, how could she explain to them that she felt reassured holding her new spring dress?

Another bomb fell, followed by rockets. The screaming and crying intensified. She held the bag with the dress in it tightly. The fighters came through the door of the building. They were wearing combat clothes. They had long beards, and on their shoulders they carried a variety of weapons. One of them rushed toward her and shouted: "Get inside the shelter! Can't you hear? Can't you see? Why are you standing here like a statue? The shelter's the only place that can protect you!" He raised his Kalashnikov and shot into the air. The panic increased, and the sound of the screaming rose up to her, but she remained motionless. The fighter became angrier. He approached her, yelling: "I told you to come down! Into the shelter! What are you doing here? Move! What's that you're clutching so nervously? Give it to me and come down!" She held the bag with her autumn-spring dress more tightly and didn't answer. The screaming rose up again, and again he yelled and shot into the air. He looked at her furiously and advanced toward her. But then she shouted: "This is my future, my autumn, my spring. I'm hanging on to it, and what I'm most afraid of is that you'll take it away from me!"

The Persian Rug
Hanan al-Shaykh

When Maryam had finished arranging my hair in two plaits, she put her finger to her mouth and licked it, then passed it over my eyebrows and sighed: "Oh, your eyebrows are so untidy!" She then turned quickly to my sister and said: "Go and see if your father has finished praying." No sooner had my sister gone than she came back and whispered: "Not yet." Imitating him, she stretched out her hands and lifted them to the sky. I didn't laugh as usual, and neither did Maryam. Instead, she took the scarf from the chair, covered her hair with it, and tied it quickly at her neck. Then she slowly opened the cabinet and took out her handbag. She put it under her arm and reached out her hands to us. I held one, and my sister held the other. We understood that we had to walk on tiptoe like her. With bated breath we went out through the open door of the house. We went down the steps, first turning our heads to the door then to the window. When we reached the last step, we started running, not stopping until the long narrow lane had disappeared from view and we had crossed the street. There Maryam stopped a cab.

We were all behaving the same way because we were afraid. Today we were going to see my mother for the first time since her divorce from my father, and he had sworn he would never let her see us again. This was because just hours after their divorce, news had come that she was going to marry the man she had loved before her family forced her to marry my father.

My heart was pounding. I knew this was not because of the fear and the running, but because I was worried about the meeting and the confusion I expected to feel. I was reserved and conscious of my shyness. However much I tried, I couldn't show my emotion, even to my mother. I wouldn't be able to throw myself into her arms and smother her with kisses, or hold her face in my hands, as my sister would, and as it was her nature to do. I had thought a long time about this, ever since Maryam had whispered to me and my sister that my mother had come back from the south and that we were going to visit her in secret the next day. At first I thought I would force myself to behave just like my sister. I would stand behind her and imitate her mechanically. Following blindly, as they say. But I knew myself. I knew myself too well. However much I tried to force myself, and however much I thought in advance about the do's and the don'ts, when the time came I would forget what I had resolved and stand looking at the floor, my eyebrows knitted even more closely together. Caught in this situation, I wouldn't despair; I would beg my lips to open into a smile—but it would be no use.

When the cab pulled up at the entrance to a house with two columns topped by two lions of red sandstone, I felt a surge of joy and momentarily forgot my fear and shyness. It delighted me that my mother lived in a house with an entrance flanked by two lions. I heard my sister imitating a lion roaring. I turned to her enviously and

The Persian Rug

saw her stretch her hands up and try to grab one of the lions. I thought to myself: "She's always so uncomplicated, so full of joy. She stays joyful even at the most critical moments. Here she is now, with no misgivings about this meeting."

When my mother opened the door and I saw her, I found I didn't have to wait for anyone else to move. I ran and threw myself into her arms, before my sister, and closed my eyes. It was as if all the joints in my body had fallen asleep after a long period of insomnia. I smelled the same old scent of her hair, and discovered for the first time how much I missed her. I wished she would come back to live with us—in spite of the love and care my father and Maryam were giving us. My thoughts wandered, recalling her smile when my father agreed to divorce her. A religious sheikh had intervened after she had threatened to douse herself in petrol and set fire to herself if the divorce didn't take place. I felt dazed from the smell of her—a smell I remembered so well. I thought about how much I missed her, even though when she had left us, with tears and kisses, we had gone back to our game in the narrow alley by our house while she had hurried off behind my uncle and climbed into the car. And when night had come, for the first time in a long time we didn't hear her quarreling with my father; silence had reigned over the house, disturbed only by Maryam's sobbing. She was related to my father and had lived with us in the house ever since I could remember.

Smiling, my mother ushered me aside so that she could hug and kiss my sister, and hug Maryam again, who had started to cry. I heard my mother say tearfully to her: "Thank you very much!" She wiped her tears away with

An Arabian Mosaic

her sleeve and, contemplating my sister and me again, exclaimed: "May God keep away the evil eye. How big you've grown!" Then she put her arms around me, and my sister put her arms around my mother's waist, and we all began to laugh when we discovered it was impossible for us to walk. We reached the inner room, and I felt sure her new husband was inside, because my mother said with a smile: "Mahmud loves you very much and wishes your father would let me have you, so that you could live with us and become his children too." Laughing, my sister answered: "You mean we're going to have two fathers?" Still dazed, I laid my hand on my mother's arm, proud of my behavior, proud of having escaped from myself and from my fettered hands and from the prison of my shyness—all without effort. I recalled the meeting with my mother, how I had spontaneously thrown myself into her arms—something I used to think was impossible—and how I had kissed her so hard that I had closed my eyes.

Her husband wasn't there. I opened my eyes, stared at the floor, then froze. Confused, I looked at the Persian rug that lay on the floor, then I looked long and hard at my mother. She didn't understand my look. She went to a cabinet, opened it, and threw me an embroidered blouse. Then she went to a decorated dressing table, took out an ivory comb painted with red hearts, and gave it to my sister. I stared at the Persian rug and trembled with resentment and anger. Again I looked at my mother. She interpreted my look as longing and affection, because she put her arms around me and said: "You must come every other day, and you must spend Fridays with me."

The Persian Rug

I remained frozen. I wanted to push her arm away. I wanted to sink my teeth into her white forearm. I wanted to go through the moment of meeting all over again: she would open the door, and I would stand as I should, looking at the floor, my eyebrows knitted together. My gaze was now resting on the Persian rug; its lines and colors were imprinted on my memory. I used to stretch out on it while studying, and find myself so close to it that I would examine its pattern. This looked like slices of red watermelon, one next to the other. When I sat on the sofa, the slices changed into combs with fine teeth. The bouquets of flowers around the four sides were purple, the color of the cockscomb. At the beginning of every summer my mother used to put mothballs on the rug—as on the rest of the rugs—then roll it up and put it on top of the cabinet. The room would look dull and sad without the rug, until autumn approached. Then my mother would climb to the roof of the house with the rug, spread it out, pick up the mothballs—most of which had dissolved from the heat and humidity of the summer—sweep the rug with a small broom, and leave it on the roof. In the evening she would fetch it down and spread it out on the floor, and I would feel overjoyed. With the rug's brighter colors, life would return to the room. But a few months before my mother's divorce, the rug had disappeared after being spread out on the roof in the sun. When my mother climbed up in the afternoon to bring it down and didn't find it, she called my father. It was the first time I saw him turn red in the face. When they came down from the roof, my mother flew into a rage. She questioned the neighbors, who swore, one after the other, that they hadn't seen the rug. Suddenly my mother cried, "Ilya!" We were all speechless—my father, myself, my sister, and our men and women neighbors. I found myself shouting: "How can you say that? It can't be true!"

Ilya was a half-blind man who frequented all the houses of the neighborhood to repair cane chairs. When our turn came, I would come home from school and find him sitting on the stone bench, his red hair shining in the sun and a pile of reeds in front of him. He would stretch out his hand and work the rush with an ease that made weaving seem like the motion of a fish slipping unharmed through the meshes of a net. I would watch him insert the rush in a hole deftly and skillfully, twist it around, and take it out again, until he had formed a circle on the seat of the chair, just like the circles before and after it. The circles were all even and alike, as if his hands were a machine. I was amazed at his speed and dexterity, and at his posture: he sat with his head inclined as if his eyes could see. Once I doubted that he could see nothing but darkness, and I found myself squatting on the ground looking up at his rosy-red face. I saw blurry eyes under his spectacles, and the white line that went through them pierced my heart. I hurried off to the kitchen, where I found a bag of dates lying on the table. I put a heap of them on a plate and gave them to Ilya.

I was still looking at the rug. The picture of Ilya, with his red hair and red face, appeared before my eyes. I saw his hand as he climbed up the steps by himself, as he sat on his chair, as he haggled, as he ate and knew he had finished everything on the plate, as he drank from the jar and the water slipped down into his throat with ease. When he came one noon, calling out "Allah!"

The Persian Rug

before knocking and entering—just as my father had taught him, in case my mother didn't have her veil on—my mother jumped at him and asked about the rug. He didn't say anything, but made a sound like crying. As he walked away, I saw him stumble for the first time, almost banging against the table. I went up to him and held his hand. He clasped it, and he recognized me by the grip of my hand, because in a voice like a whisper he said to me: "Never mind, girl." Then he turned to leave. When he leaned down to put his shoes on, I thought I saw little tears on his cheeks. My father said: "God will forgive you, Ilya, if you tell the truth." But Ilya walked away, supporting himself on the rails of the stairway. He went down the steps, taking time—unusually—to feel his way along. Finally he disappeared, and we never saw him again.

The Picture
Nawal al-Saadawi

Everything could have gone on as before in Nargis's life, had her hand not collided accidentally with Nabawiyya's backside, and had her fingers not hit a soft curve of flesh, and had her amazed eyes not seen a pair of small protrusions wobbling along under Nabawiyya's dress in time with the jerking of her arms as she stood washing at the sink. She had realized for the first time that Nabawiyya had buttocks. Nabawiyya, who had come to them from the country a year ago, a little servant, her body thin, dry like a stick of corn; you could hardly tell her back from her front, and had it not been for her name you would have thought her a boy.

Nargis found herself by the mirror in her room, and she turned around in front of it. Her eyes opened wide in amazement when she saw a pair of small protrusions shaking under her dress. She stretched out her hand inquisitively, exploring her backside. Her trembling fingers came across a pair of soft spheres of flesh. Was she growing buttocks too?

She lifted up her dress from the back to reveal them, then twisted her head to see them from the other side, but they turned as her body turned and disappeared behind it. She tried to steady her lower half in front of the mirror and look right round it, but she couldn't.

An Arabian Mosaic

When her head turned, the upper part of her body turned with it, and when that happened, the lower half of her body followed. She felt slightly baffled. She could see Nabawiyya from the rear, but not herself. At that moment she imagined she had discovered a new misfortune for man—that he could see other people's bodies but not the body in which he himself was born and which he carried around with him everywhere, and all the time.

An idea flashed across her mind: to go to the kitchen and ask Nabawiyya to look at her from the rear and describe her buttocks to her precisely. What shape were they? Were they round or oval? Did they shake when she was standing still or only when she walked? Did they protrude and attract attention or didn't they?

She set off, but then she stopped. Could she ask Nabawiyya something like that? Nabawiyya the servant, with whom she never spoke? She would give her orders, which hardly resembled speech, and Nabawiyya's answers, consisting of "okay or "yes," hardly resembled speech either. They were spontaneous reactions, coming out regularly at a speed and pitch reminiscent of the vibrations of a machine, each sound the same as the next.

She felt slightly angry, and she resolved to get to see her rear by her own efforts. She pulled up her dress and bared herself completely from the back. Then she steadied her legs on the floor, twisted her head, and moved her eyes round across her body. Before long her head stopped moving, her eyes not managing the full sweep round her body. She strained her muscles and tried once more to twist her head. She had her head turned in front of the mirror and her rear completely bared, when her

The Picture

gaze met that of her father's, and she shuddered. She knew they were not his real eyes, only his picture hanging on the wall, but her little body continued to tremble until she had pulled the dress down and covered up her rear. She couldn't take her eyes off his. She wanted to see them. Every time she looked at her father she felt she was not seeing enough of him, that she wanted to see more of him. For thirteen years, from the time she was born, she had seen him every day only from the back. When he had his back to her, she could raise her eyes and contemplate his tall, broad figure. She never looked him in the eye, and never exchanged a glance or a word with him. When he looked at her, she bowed her head; and if he spoke to her, it was not words he uttered, but instructions and orders, to which she responded with "okay" or "yes" mechanically, in blind obedience. When he told her to leave school and stay at home, she left school and stayed at home. When he told her not to open the windows, she didn't open the windows. When he told her not to look from behind the shutters, she didn't look from behind the shutters. Even when he told her to perform ablutions before going to sleep, so that she would dream noble dreams, she began performing the ablutions and dreaming noble dreams.

Her eyes were still drawn to his. She wanted to look at him without bowing her head, to fix her eyes on his eyes and see them, know them, get acquainted with them. But she couldn't. There was always a distance separating her eyes from his; and she was unable to see them close up, even though her nose was almost touching the picture. His head looked big, his nose large and crooked, and his eyes sunken, wide, almost swallowing her up. She hid her face in her hands. A picture of the big desk flashed across her mind, and behind it her father's crooked nose rising from among the many papers. From time to time he would look at the long line of people standing in front of him, gazing at him pleadingly, submissively. His big head would move between the piles of papers, his long, thick fingers twisted around the pen as it raced across the paper. She would pull her slim little legs together as she sat in the corner, and withdraw within herself, trying to breathe quietly. Could she really be the daughter of this great man? When her father stood up, his tall, broad figure rose high behind the desk, and his nose almost touched the ceiling. She carried her head proudly as she walked beside him on the street; she could almost see the eyes all directed at her father, and the lips all opened in good wishes for him. Her little ears could almost catch the soft whisper that always went around among the passers-by on the street: "This is the master of authority and intelligence, and this is his daughter, Nargis, who walks at his side!" And when the two of them crossed the street, her father would hold her hand in his hand, and turn his big fingers around her little fingers, and her heart would pound, and her breaths would follow each other in quick succession, and she would bend her head to kiss his hand. As soon as her hand touched his big hairy hand, that powerful smell would reach her nose— the distinctive smell of her father. She didn't know exactly what it was, but she smelled it wherever he was; and when she went into his room she smelled it in all the corners, in the bed, in the wardrobe, and in the clothes. Sometimes she would bury her head in his clothes in order to smell it even more; she would kiss his clothes

The Picture

and stroke them and kneel in front of the big picture of him above his bed, almost praying. Not the usual prayer which she would perform quickly to a god she never saw, but a real act of worship to a real god whom she could see with her own eyes, hear with her own ears, and smell with her own nose. He was the one who bought food and clothes for her, and had a huge desk and lots of papers, and knew the contents of all of them, and provided for people's needs, and most importantly, wrote with a pen at eye-dazzling speed.

Nargis found herself kneeling in front of the picture as if in prayer. She rose, her head bowed low in humility, and kissed his hand, as was her custom every night before she went to sleep. As she lay on her back, her protruding buttocks rubbed against the bed, and a new, pleasant quiver shook her body. She stretched out her trembling fingers to feel her backside. Two rounded lumps of flesh gathered between her and the bed. She turned over onto her face to stop herself feeling them and to try to sleep, but they rose up into the air, their weight pressing down on her stomach. She turned over onto her side, but they continued to rub against the bed every time she breathed in or out. She held her breath for a moment, but the breathing soon began again, the breaths sending rapid jolts through her little body, and shaking the bed in time with themselves, causing it to squeak softly. It seemed to her that in the silence of the night the squeaking was audible, that it would reach her father's ears as he slept in his room, and that he would know for sure where it came from and what caused it.

She shuddered at the thought and tried to suppress her breaths so that the bed would stop squeaking; she almost choked, but the air burst inside her chest, and her body shook violently, and with it the bed, emitting its harsh squeaking in the silence of the night. Finally she jumped out of the bed.

As soon as she set her feet on the floor, the bed stopped squeaking and all she could then hear was the sound of her breaths, one after the other. Little by little, they began to calm down, eventually becoming completely quiet. The customary silence had hardly returned to her room, when she remembered that she hadn't performed the usual ablutions before going to bed. Having discovered the cause of all the sinful sensations that had stolen into her impure body, she relaxed a little.

While she was standing in front of the sink, performing her ablutions, uttering the invocation "In the name of God, the Beneficent, the Merciful," pronouncing the formula "There is no power and no strength save in God," and seeking refuge in God from the accursed Satan, she heard a low noise coming from behind the kitchen door. Was Nabawiyya only just going to bed? She pushed gently on the kitchen door, but it didn't open. Once more she heard the low noise, so she put her ear to the door and clearly heard the sound of confused and rapid breathing. She smiled, relaxing a little. Nabawiyya was awake like her, exploring her new buttocks! She moved her head unconsciously toward the door, and her eyes came to rest on the keyhole. She peeped into the kitchen. The small sofa on which Nabawiyya slept was empty, and something was moving on the kitchen floor. She looked closely. Her eyes opened wide as her gaze settled on a naked two-headed heap of flesh rolling about on the floor. One of the heads, with its long plaits,

The Picture

was Nabawiyya's, and the other, with its high, crooked nose, was her father's! At that moment she could have fallen to the floor, far away from the keyhole, but her eyes remained there, glued fast to it, as if a part of it. Her gaze froze on the big naked heap as it rolled about, as Nabawiyya's head came down onto the floor, bumping against the garbage can, and as her father's head rose up and hit the bottom of the sink. But they had soon swapped positions, and it was Nabawiyya's head that was hitting the bottom of the sink, and her father's head that was striking the garbage can. Before long, both heads had disappeared under the shelf where the cooking pots were kept, and she could no longer see anything but four legs, with their twenty toes jerking rapidly; some of the toes were entangled with others, making a strange shape, like a water creature with many arms, or an octopus.

Nargis didn't know how she managed to tear her eyes away from the keyhole, or how she had got back to her room to look in the mirror. Her little head was trembling as her gaze jerked quickly over her body. Her wandering eyes fell on her protruding buttocks, moving in time with the rapid jolting of the rest of her body. Unconsciously, she stretched out her hand and bared her rear, looking at her father's picture out of the corner of her eye. She almost felt the same old shudder go through her arms, and she almost pulled down her dress to cover herself. But her arms didn't move, and she kept staring at her father's face without bowing her head. His wide eyes were bulging, and his sharp, crooked nose sliced his face in two. A long cobweb clung to the end of the high pointed nose, moving to and fro in the night breeze that was rushing in through the shutters.

    Nargis went up to the picture and blew on the cobweb to clear it away, but drops of her spittle spread over the picture, and the web stuck to her father's face. Again she tried to blow it away, but it only stuck on all the more. She stretched out her hand unconsciously, and with her long sharp nails began to rub the spider's long thin threads off the picture. She managed to remove them, but at the same time she had destroyed the picture, which had become wet with her spittle, and it fell from between her fingers to the floor in little fragments . . .

The Picture
Latifa al-Zayat

Amal's eyes settled on a splash of wave that moved on the horizon, leaving behind a spiral lit up in rainbow colors by the sun's rays. It was a wonderful rainbow, visible only if you tilted your head at a certain angle and looked hard. She pointed the rainbow out to her husband, who was sitting across the table from her in the casino overlooking the point where the Nile meets the sea at Ras al-Barr. He couldn't see it. If only he could see it. The rainbow seemed to disappear when it was still there, and seemed still to be there when it had already disappeared with the waves as they pulled away from the rocks of the Tongue, stretching out where sea and river meet. Once again the waves would come and thrust against the rocks, and again the rainbow would rise up. Amal cried out in delight:

"There it is, Izzat, there it is!"

Her son, Midhat, grabbed the hem of her dress and followed her gaze:

"Where, Mama, where?"

The look of boredom evaporated from Izzat's eyes, and he burst out laughing. A man in a turban, wearing a full suit and waistcoat, shouted: "Double five, my dear sir, double five," and he brought the chips down onto the backgammon board. The fat man who was playing with him swallowed hard and pulled at the opening of his white cotton-and-silk gown, wiping away the sweat. An old photographer wearing a black suit took hold of his boy and shook him as he sat fast asleep, propped up against the developing bucket. Brushing the sand off his bare feet, the man selling raffle tickets shouted: "You never know your luck!"

Amal smiled her shy, apologetic smile. The contagious laughter took hold of her and she burst out laughing without knowing why. Suddenly she stopped, realizing she was happy.

Midhat asked for ice cream, and Izzat was turning to look for the waiter when his gaze halted, glued to the casino entrance. He smiled, drawing down his thick lip, on which moisture had appeared; his hand moved unconsciously to open another button on his white shirt, uncovering more of the copious hair on his chest.

The table behind Amal was now occupied by a woman in her thirties, wearing shorts that exposed her full, white legs, her dyed blond hair wrapped in a red georgette scarf with white jasmine; with her sat another woman in her fifties, wearing a dress that revealed a tanned and wrinkled cleavage. Izzat clapped his hands, shouting loudly for the waiter, although he was nearby and just a sign would have done:

"Three, three ice creams."

Amal was alarmed by her husband's unusual lavishness. She whispered, blushing:

"Two's enough, Izzat. I don't feel like any."

Izzat seemed not to hear her. He repeated, in a feverish voice:

The Picture

"Three ice creams of mixed flavors. Have you got that?"

When the waiter moved away, he called to him again, enunciating every word:

"Make one of them vanilla. Yes, vanilla ice cream."

Amal smiled triumphantly as she relaxed in her seat.

"Where will you get the money from? Where will you get the money to go on summer vacation?" her mother had said. "From the fifteen pounds he takes home every month? You've been putting money aside. That's why your hands are chapped from washing. That's why you've lost weight. If only he was a decent man who understood and appreciated what you do. But he neglects you like a dog, and goes fooling around . . ."

Amal pressed her lips together in an ironic expression. She and Izzat were finally together, the whole time, on vacation, at the hotel in Ras al-Barr. Fifteen days without cooking or cleaning, without the intense heat or waiting up for him. She leaned her head back proudly, pushing away a lock of pitch-black hair from her tawny forehead. She noticed Izzat's eyes and felt a lump in her throat.

The fire was burning in Izzat's eyes again. Those eyes, which for a long time were unseeing, gliding over things without stopping, had begun to perceive. They were once again lit with that fire, fascinating and bewildering at the same time, the fire that burned and begged. Had she forgotten that gaze of his? Or had she deliberately tried to forget it so as not to miss it? The important thing was that it had come back, as if there had been no yesterday without it. Was it the summer resort? Was it the vacation? What mattered was that it had come back to envelop her with fever again. Amal noticed Izzat's dark brown hand, with its protruding veins, and she was racked with a desire to lean over and kiss it. Her eyes filled with tears. She drew Midhat close to her with groping hands and planted kisses on him from cheek to ear. She hugged him, and when the fire that had invaded her body had subsided, she let him go and began searching for the rainbow through her tears, tilting her head to the side.

She must be sure. Was that really the rainbow or was it the rainbow of her tears? . . . "Tomorrow you'll cry blood instead of tears," her mother had said, and her father had added: "You're young, my daughter, and tomorrow love and these empty words will go away and nothing will remain except misery . . ." Amal shook her head as if to dislodge a fly that had landed on her cheek, and muttered to herself: "You don't understand anything. I found what I had been looking for all my life." She held the rainbow in her gaze, then woke up to a metallic cracking sound, as the ice-cream glasses chafed against the marble of the table.

"Three ice creams, two mixed and one vanilla."

"The vanilla's for me, sir, the vanilla's enough for me."

Izzat enunciated the words carefully, smiling a meaningful smile in a certain direction. Which direction? A lewd female laugh replied. Was it a reply to the smile? Amal encircled the frosty glass with her hands, then turned round, watching him. *Strawberry, pistachio . . . and the yellow? Mango? Apricot? Dye, just dye . . . It can't be . . . It can't be . . .*

"Come on, eat up," Izzat cajoled her.

Amal picked up the spoon and drew it close to the ice

The Picture

cream, but then she put it back in its place and encircled the glass with her hands once again. Izzat directed the conversation to Midhat:

"Is the ice cream tasty, Midhat?"

"Yes, tasty."

"Tasty like you are, my darling."

Another burst of laughter rang out behind her. Amal's hands stiffened on the frosty glass, from which cold steam was rising, like smoke. She lifted her eyes and turned her head without moving her shoulders, in order to scrutinize the woman in shorts. She did it reluctantly, slowly, fearing someone might see her, fearing Izzat might spot her action. And then she saw her . . . *white as a plastered wall . . . as a candle . . . as vanilla ice cream?!* Amal's eyes met the woman's for a fleeting second, and her lower lip trembled. Her gaze fell back onto the ice-cream glass; she lifted her head and shoulders and sat stiffly, eating.

The woman in shorts took a cigarette out of her bag and left it dangling from her lips until the woman with the naked cleavage lit it for her. She began puffing its smoke provocatively toward Amal. But Amal didn't look round at her. *The woman's cheap. Izzat only has to open his mouth and she laughs. Cheap, no doubt about that. It's not fair to Izzat.*

Midhat finished eating his ice cream and started shifting around from boredom. His lips curled up, as if he was on the point of crying:

"The Tongue . . . I want to go to the Tongue."

Amal sighed, a great worry had been removed, relief had come. This cheap woman would vanish from her sight forever. She leaned her head to the side, smiling, and, carefully enunciating the words as if playing a role in front of crowds of spectators, she said:

"Of course, my darling . . . straight away. Mama and Papa will take Midhat and go to the Tongue."

Amal pushed back her chair, laughing briefly as she got ready to stand up. Then Izzat said in an unduly harsh tone:

"Where to?"

"The boy wants to go to the Tongue."

"And after the Tongue where shall we go? Are we going to stifle ourselves in the hotel from now on?"

Midhat burst out crying, striking against the floor with his feet. Amal jumped up nervously to hold him. *Izzat? Izzat wants to sit here because . . . It can't be . . . God, it can't be.* Midhat was alarmed at the force of her grip, and his crying intensified.

"Shut up!" screamed Izzat.

Midhat didn't shut up, so Izzat jumped up and pulled him out of his mother's arms, hit him twice on the hand, then sat down, saying, as if justifying his position to others:

"I won't tolerate a whining child."

Amal went back to her seat. The tears flowed silently from Midhat's eyes, gathering at the corner of his mouth. Then the woman in shorts said, in a hoarse, drawn-out voice, as if she had just woken up:

"Come on, sweetheart, come to me."

And out of her pocket she took a piece of chocolate in a red wrapping.

"Come on, darling, come take the chocolate."

Amal pulled Midhat toward her. The woman in shorts leaned her head to the side, crossed her legs, and smiled

The Picture

slightly as she threw the chocolate onto the table within Midhat's view. Amal rested Midhat's head against her chest and began to stroke his hair with trembling hands. Midhat let himself be cradled by his mother for a moment, then he lifted his arm to wipe away his tears and started to steal glances from under it at the chocolate. The woman in shorts signaled to Midhat and winked sideways at him. Amal buried Midhat's head in her chest. *It can't be . . . He can't possibly go to her . . . Izzat . . . Midhat . . . Izzat can't be ogling her.* Midhat made a sudden movement, slipped out of his mother's grip, and ran to the adjacent table. The lewd laugh rang out again, triumphant, reverberating.

Amal, her lips turning blue, whispered:

"Go and get the boy."

Izzat smiled defiantly:

"Why don't you go and get him yourself?"

Amal's voice choked:

"We're not beggars."

"What's begging got to do with it? Surely you don't want the boy to become as shy as you are!"

Amal didn't look round at the table behind her, where her son was sitting on the lap of the woman in shorts, eating chocolate and smudging his mouth and his chin and his hands and his shirt. She wished she could grab him and hit him till . . . But what fault was it of his? The fault was hers alone. The woman in shorts said in her hoarse, drawn-out voice:

"Bravo. We've finished the chocolate. Now we'll go and wash our hands."

Amal jumped to her feet, her face pale. The woman in shorts walked away with a swinging gait, dragging Midhat behind her. Speaking softly, his hand on Amal's shoulder, Izzat said:

"You stay here. I'll get the boy."

Amal remained standing, watching them, the woman holding Midhat by the hand, the woman with Izzat behind her. She watched them as they crossed the outer balcony of the casino, then through the glass, as they crossed the inner hall and disappeared inside the building. The woman's buttocks were swinging as if disconnected from her, and behind her went Izzat, his body leaning forward, as if he were about to charge. On they went, step after step, step close to step, step clinging to step. Amal's hand stretched out unconsciously to wipe away drops of sweat that had gathered at the corner of her mouth.

"No Izzat, not like that . . . You're frightening me . . . You're frightening me like that, Izzat . . ." She had said these words as she collapsed onto a rock in the cavern at the Aquarium. It was during their courtship. Izzat was gasping: "Oh Amal, if you could only imagine how much I love you." His lips curled up, his eyes were half-closed, giving him the look of a cat calling its mate, a look that burned and begged. *Izzat and the other woman?! Izzat wanting to . . . It's not possible . . . It's not possible . . .*

"A picture, madam?"

Amal fell onto the chair in exhaustion, signaling to the old photographer to go away. "No Izzat, don't put your hand on my neck like that . . . What will people say when they see the picture?" "They'll say I love you, Amal." "No, don't, really." "There it is, my lady, the picture came out with my hand on your neck, and now

The Picture

you won't be able to get away from me, ever." That was what he had said that day, victorious.

"A postcard picture for ten piasters, and no waiting, madam."

"Later, later," Amal replied, annoyed.

The old photographer walked away, repeating in a dull, listless chant: "Family pictures, souvenir pictures." Behind him the barefoot man selling raffle tickets wiped his hand on his khaki pants and called out: "You never know your luck! Three numbers and we'll draw. A valuable Chinese tea set for just one piaster. It's a giveaway!" Amal lifted her hand from the table, the chill of the marble had suddenly stung her.

"I'm lucky, Mother. I married a real man." "You married a loose man," her mother had said. "Work! Is that what he says, work?! It's a strange office that stays open till one and two o'clock in the morning!" Their neighbor Saber Effendi had said as much as Sit Saniyya was pouring out the coffee. "My dear child, Saber Effendi has been in government service for forty years, and nothing happens that he doesn't know about."

Izzat came back with Midhat. Sitting him down on his lap, he said softly:

"The boy took ages. He didn't want to wash his hands."

Amal gave him a scrutinizing, cold look, as if seeing him for the first time. Then she turned her face away and focused her gaze on a stain left on Midhat's shirt from the chocolate. Izzat seemed completely absorbed in teaching Midhat how to count from one to ten. Midhat stretched out his hand and shut his father's mouth. Izzat smiled and, leaning toward Amal, said:

An Arabian Mosaic

"You know you look very attractive today. Pink really suits you."

She felt a lump in her throat and she smiled faintly. The old photographer repeated:

"A group picture, sir? It'll be very nice, and you get it right away."

"No, thank you," said Izzat.

Amal noticed the woman in shorts coming along, with her swinging gait. In a choked voice she said:

"Let's have a picture taken."

"What for?" protested Izzat.

The other woman passed her, aloof, not looking at her or at Izzat. She sat down in her chair and became engrossed in a conversation with her friend. Amal leaned toward Izzat, and the words came out of her mouth in a whisper, choked:

"Let's have our picture taken, you and me . . . Let's . . ." She pointed a finger at him, a finger at herself, then joined the two fingers together. Izzat shrugged his shoulders and said resignedly:

"Take a picture, fellow."

As the photographer put his head under the black cover, Amal stretched out her hand and grabbed her husband's arm; and when the photographer gave the signal, her hand tightened its grip. While waiting for the photo to be developed, Izzat didn't look at the woman, and the woman didn't look at him. When the photographer came back with the picture, Izzat got up, looking for change.

Amal seized the picture eagerly and held it firmly in her hands, as if afraid someone would snatch it from her . . . *Izzat at her side . . . her darling . . . her husband.*

The Picture

The woman in shorts stood up, pushing her chair back violently. When she passed by the adjacent table, her eyes met Amal's for a brief moment—a fleeting moment, but sufficient—and Amal let the picture fall from her hands.

It fell to the ground a little way from her. Without moving from her place, she leaned her elbows on her thighs and her head on her hands, and began to scrutinize the picture with a cold, expressionless face. The picture of a strange woman looked up at her, a feverish woman feverishly gripping the arm of a man whose face reflected the pain of the violent grip. Slowly and calmly Amal stretched out her leg, and with the toe of her shoe, then with the heel, defaced the picture. She drew her leg back and bent her head, scrutinizing the picture once again.

The sand had obliterated the main features, but some parts remained clear: the man's face, with its expression of pain, and the woman's hand, clutching the man's arm. Once more Amal stretched out her leg, and with the toe of her shoe drew the picture close to her chair, till it was within arm's reach. Then she bent down and picked it up.

When Izzat came back with the change, the picture had turned into small pieces blowing about in the wind. And the rainbow had disappeared. The sun reached midpoint in the sky, and people were running so that the hot sand would not burn their feet.

Amal realized that there was a long road ahead of her . . .

The Picture
Layla al-Uthman

My birthday party was over. A woman of forty-five celebrating her birthday . . .

I looked around me. The blue night had become completely still. Groups of people were stealing away, one by one, going their own separate ways. Some guests had left their good sense at the bottom of their glasses and staggered out happily. Chaos reigned over the room, waiting for the morning, when the servant's hands would work to clear it up. Paper decorations, silver and golden, lay scattered about or hung from the ceiling like lifeless caterpillars.

Empty, dry glasses stood as tokens of the avid thirst of those who had held them. Others contained half-melted ice. The ice mixed with what was in the glass till the smell of the drinker's mouth seemed to emanate from the concoction. The table was overflowing with leftovers, most of which lay there spoiled, untouched. Perhaps the visitors had suffered an attack of indigestion—they had a habit of overindulgence. Every small table had on it several bowls full of cigarette and cigar butts. The contents gave off a strange aroma. Some people hate it, but I had always liked it. It gave me a dazed feeling, sending a kind of longing through my body for a moment of evening rest.

An Arabian Mosaic

Alone . . .

I stood in front of the big mirror with the golden frame. It gleamed. My face and half my body were reflected in it. I drew closer, closer, until my face filled the mirror. I looked at it closely. It was only then that I decided to be unfaithful to my husband.

I wasn't taken by any of the faces at the party, nor daunted by them, despite the fact that the fronts of some women's dresses revealed cleavage that resembled the warm course of a river, emanating smells of splendid fragrances. Some of the perfumes I liked, others I had an aversion to. This aversion developed with the craving that accompanied my first pregnancy, and it has persisted to this day.

The men sidled up and sniffed, lust and hunger in their glances, forgetting they were in someone else's home. Friendships formed, and perhaps with a single glance it was agreed on a time and a place.

No face stirred me, except the one I was now following . . . my husband's face: his wrinkled forehead, and the two deep furrows dividing the space between his eyes like two juxtaposed numbers, giving the face a wickedness alien to my husband; his body, tall and full; his hair, thin at the front and thick at the temples, like a halo of snow on a wintery night; his long nose, scattered with a few old scars; and his big lips, the upper one half-covered by a thick, silvery mustache.

My husband's face excited my curiosity. The smile, the thoughtfulness, sometimes the hardness and distractedness, and a lot of charm.

And what about my own face, which I was now looking at in the mirror? The mirror was reflecting the truth to me. The damned mirror was gloating over me, as if saying:

"This is you, and this is the truth you're trying to ignore." *I'm a woman of forty-five and my husband is still intent on celebrating my birthday, as if I were still a little child, a young girl. Perhaps he loves me. Or perhaps he does it to remind me that the years are passing, one by one, coming and going and eating away my life, year after year, carrying away with them freshness and vitality and youth and beauty.*

My face was not terribly ugly, but of course it was less charming and attractive than my husband's. Wrinkles surrounded my eyes—unlike his eyes, around which the skin was still tight, although he was over fifty-three.

This was my face, and that was its truth. A truth that suddenly provoked a strange feeling of rebellion in my soul.

I made a resolution: to be unfaithful to my husband.

How? When? With whom? I wasn't concerned with finding answers to these serious questions. I was at a moment of resolution. I resolved to embark on an experience—I felt I needed it. An experience that would bring back feelings of youth. A woman of forty-five, but desired, longed for. She has another man. He dreams of her, thinks about her, cares for her. Just like those other women, the ones who attracted my husband's attention. Perhaps they had engaged him in a moment of fleeting pleasure, or perhaps the relationship had lasted several months without my knowing. After all, I was confident of my appeal and attractiveness.

Tonight was unlike any other night—it was the beginning of a new journey over mental horizons. It would transfer me from my husband to the embrace of another man whose features I didn't know yet. Who *was* that man I was now deciding to be unfaithful to my husband with?

    I buried myself in the blanket. It was cold. My husband had fallen asleep before me and was snoring. Every time he breathed out, his mustache trembled. His eyes were relaxed, and the furrows between them had separated a little and become less deep.

    I felt cold biting my fingertips. I thought of moving closer to him. I would slip my feet under his warm legs. But I drew back. For a moment something strange tormented me. What a coward I was, resolving secretly to embark for the first time on a journey my husband wouldn't share. I was moving away from him, disengaging myself, making a strange decision, without any feeling of the hideousness of what I was contemplating. Then I felt rebellion surge up inside me again, disrupting my calm, rebuking me. Why shouldn't I have another man? He would become part of my life. I would meet him the day my husband left me for another, younger woman. He, of course, had no thought of having a younger woman—as a standby—since he could find one whenever he wanted. There were many women available out there, waiting for a signal. But I was a woman who needed a long time to build a bridge between herself and a man, a woman cautious in her choice, who didn't rush into things, and didn't beg a man.

    I stopped, wondering. Who could I replace my husband with when his desire died out? What kind of relationship was I capable of developing with the person?

The Picture

And could I guarantee that my husband would not find out about the affair?

I looked at him again. This man, asleep, his head resting on the pillow, recovering from the hardships of the day. Was he not dreaming about what I was thinking?

What of me? What stupidity had got into me? Shouldn't I be ashamed of all this idle talk—a woman who had bid farewell to her forty-fifth year?

In the morning I felt the urge to return to the previous day's unsuccessful debate. My resolution began to challenge my mind, and my conscience.

I reviewed the names of other men linked to me by chance or necessity. I also reviewed the names of my husband's many men friends. Why shouldn't I? Perhaps he had had some kind of experience with one of my women friends. But I didn't find a single face amongst them that my soul desired, and none of them set that cord of longing stirring in me.

I became very calm. Only my mind was active. I felt a continuous sense of rebellion. I was driven by boredom, drawn from one room to another, from wardrobe to drawer. I searched for something to do. All the things that might need tidying up or dusting suddenly looked in perfect order. I loathed everything around me. The house was rejecting me. I decided to go out.

I got into the car in a state of bewilderment. The makeup I had plastered on my face the previous evening still lingered in the furrows, filling them.

The sun was hot, burning my face. It felt as if it were melting the oil in my face cream, and the gold eyeshadow.

I felt reckless. A woman looking for some kind of

adventure, some frivolous dream; looking for something inside her soul to restore her confidence and tranquility. But I could find nothing, and I unleashed the fury of my failure on the gas pedal. The car flew along, defying everything, even the stoplights.

I stopped at the central market. My eye chanced on a face. I turned away from it. It was not the face I wanted, not even to chance on. My gaze crossed many others. But the faces were ordinary. They didn't stir anything in the soul of a woman who wanted a man. A man whose description she herself could not give.

Hurrying into the market, I collided with someone and stood back to apologize. *Oh, that face! Haven't I seen it before? Where was it?* I stared at it inquisitively, attracting the other person's attention.

Did I really know that face?

I was certain I had met this woman before. A woman approaching fifty, whose face I knew so well. *Oh God!* The woman looked at me with a mixture of anger and amazement. She moved away from me, but her face lingered in my memory.

I roamed around the market, laden with all sorts of things I didn't need, my mind elsewhere. Where had I seen her?

Suddenly I remembered a picture of a woman. It had come with one of the letters that my son, who was studying abroad, used to send me, telling me news about himself, and even about his adventures with women. The letter had said:

"Please, Mother, don't be angry. I've spent an unforgettable night with a middle-aged woman. She likes to enjoy herself like a young person, even though her own

The Picture

young days are over for good. I was traveling by train from my city to another city far away. There's a festival of flowers there every year at this time. The people there love flowers, Mother, and hold a festival to celebrate them. You know how fond I am of flowers . . . and of 'beauties.'

"This woman sat near me. She chatted to me about her young days. To be honest, although she was rather silly, what she said was amusing, especially when she told me about her marriage, and her husband, and her awful life with him. She really made me forget the long journey. And after that she made me miss my return train. And then she was inviting me to spend the night with her.

"I'm used to drinking a lot. And with her I drank a little more than usual. The drink took control of me, and the woman got drunk as well, and lost what sense she had. I suddenly found myself embracing the flabby body on top of an antique rug. She had told me about this rug on the train, stressing the price she had paid for it and how she had competed with others to buy it. I don't know how many men before me had slept on this rug. Anyway, I did my duty. When I had had a rest, things started coming back to me. I felt disgusted: her body was sweaty and her joints bony, and there was a smell of old age from the parts of her body that were untouched by cosmetics. I had irrigated a dead land . . . I asked myself: How long is it since this 'antique' has touched a man's body? In any event, it was an experience. And when she said goodbye to me at the station, she made a point of giving me her picture, smiling and saying:

83

An Arabian Mosaic

'Maybe you'll remember me, and come back soon.' And so as *not* to remember her, I'm sending *you* her picture."

Oh . . . her picture . . . I turned around, looking for the face of the woman I had bumped into. I didn't find it. I felt anger flare up in my chest as the picture haunted my imagination.

I dashed out of the central market and flung my trembling body into the car, which by then was as hot as a furnace. I put my foot down nervously on the gas pedal. The features of my face, even the smallest details of my body, flashed across my mind . . . In the rearview mirror, I saw a car. In it was a familiar face. I slowed down . . . As I drove away, I gradually forgot the woman's face, and so . . . the picture.

The Lady with the Story
May Ziyada

Everyone has a basic story. Relatives and distant relations tell it to each other in their various dialects; they understand it according to their different mentalities, and weave a host of tales around it. One person cites the basic story about his chosen victim on a particular occasion, then adds: "And he played this trick on me!" and "There was the saga with my colleague, and that episode with someone else," and so on. The narrator is lavish with this "story," explaining it, going into great detail about it, embellishing it, adorning it. And the others listen in amazement, tut-tutting and invoking the Almighty. They poke fun and jeer, as if neither they nor anyone before them had ever done anything like what is being related to them. Naturally, when they apply the rules to others, they don't see how lax they are in judging themselves. Yet the golden principle of loving your neighbor and treating others as you wish to be treated yourself is still a golden principle. There's no getting away from it.

When judging others, people don't follow the criteria they apply to themselves. They judge according to the rigid texts that make up the moral code, using these as ammunition against each other. If faults are put up for auction, it's an auction where competition to determine the lowest bidder is precluded. The speakers, whose capacity as such makes them righteous, pure, and pre-eminently saintly, turn to this severe code with the look of executioners. Just as the arithmetic table that the Greek Pythagoras invented provides us with a ready reckoner, so the moral code provides us with a way of reckoning up the evil deeds of the servants of God, and judging them. It's a ready reckoner whose sublime numerals are above any dubious deduction!

* * *

I used to meet the lady Gh. B. frequently in various places: at church, at concerts, and in department stores. I rarely walked through the streets of the Ismailiyya quarter—for example, Qasr al-Nil Street, or Imad al-Din, or al-Maghribi, or al-Madabigh, or Sulayman Pasha—without seeing her pass by, so that it seemed she must live in one of these districts or nearby. If I was with a friend or companion, up would go the cry that usually goes up amongst women—and men too, with due respect to our honorable gentlemen—when a lady with some distinguishing feature passes by: "Look! Look!" And this particular lady had more than one distinguishing feature. She was known for her beautiful voice—I had heard her sing at two parties—and she dressed elegantly, in the most up-to-date clothes. In fact, she was among the first to popularize the latest fashions in Cairo. And she was known as a beauty.

    I used to watch her from a distance, attracted to her by that special thing that is in all human beings. It's not their clothes, or their facial features, or the way they move, or their silence; it's something indefinable, some-

The Lady with the Story

thing that differs with each individual. Some observers of physiognomy maintain that it's located between the eyes; others say it's in the pupil of the eye, or around the mouth, or in the line of the lips, or in the tilt of the chin. I only know that it's there, and that it's the greatest definer of what we call "the personality of the individual." With some people it's very strong and has a great impact. It seizes the onlooker, and after that they can never forget this "personality" or its bearer.

Once the words "Look!" "Look!" have been uttered, there inevitably follows a "story" about the subject under scrutiny. That's how I came to hear many stories about the lady in question, stories that made me think a lot about her. I asked myself what other "special qualities" she had. What should I believe from all the gossip? My preoccupation with her increased as the stories about her mounted up. I was like the man who was introduced to a celebrity and said: "I've heard all the bad things people say about you, and I couldn't wait to get to know such a formidable person."

Her eyes were the thing that stuck most firmly in my mind. They were ever changing. Sometimes they looked like the eyes of a woman in pain, a long-suffering woman; and sometimes they were contemplative, avoiding all the show of life. Sometimes they had an unfathomable look: they pierced through things into the surrounding space, as if they were watching the signs of an invisible hand in the air. And sometimes they seemed like the eyes of a gregarious person who enjoys the usual festivities and is quite content with them, not imagining that anything better exists. At these times they shone, happy, as if life had given them their fill of quiet delight, and was realizing its highest hopes through them. But I liked them when they became dull and the light in them went out, as if their owner had aged fifty years in two weeks. Then I would meet her another time, and, in her rose-colored dress, with her hat fluttering around her face, she would seem like a child, anticipating all sorts of joys from life.

* * *

One day the cream of the city's amateur musicians arranged a musical gathering in the big festival hall at the Shepherd Hotel. Two famous professors supervised its organization. One was Lady K., the most talented of the foreign singing teachers. She held meetings at her home, and those who studied under her and moved in her circle—the finest men and women singers of Cairo—flocked to them. The other was Signore F., who had lived in the city for years and had numerous male and female students from various colonies of foreigners. He regularly performed such miracles on the piano that the number of his friends and admirers grew steadily.

At this gathering, the lady with the story sang. But I couldn't find anyone who could tell me anything about her—perhaps because most of the people present were amateurs. Every time a player played, or a singer sang, they all rushed to congratulate his or her relatives, thus guaranteeing they would also be congratulated when their children sang and played. The woman didn't have any family, yet her singing created a big stir and provoked loud applause, which she accepted with simple silence. A deep, jet-black flame appeared in her eyes; she had the look of a woman who is neither young nor

The Lady with the Story

old, like a statue, with unchanging features and unvarying posture.

I thought about her for a long time that evening, and from all that I had heard about her I pieced together a painful story. Then I said to myself: "What a waste! Why does this woman pretend not to know her true self? Why doesn't she forget she's a beautiful woman and rise to the level I'm sure she merits?"

The next morning Signore F. came to give me my music lesson. Instead of arriving at eleven o'clock—which was the appointed time—he arrived at ten minutes before noon. He came in, rubbing his hands, his eyes shining behind his spectacles. I grumbled: "Professor, you don't care about my time! You've ruined my morning. In fact, you've ruined my whole day!" He laughed; it was a laugh which began moderately but ended in a sound like the chirping of birds. "I'm not a mathematics teacher," he said. "I'm not obliged to come at the appointed time." And he rubbed his hands again, citing a French proverb to the effect that some disorder is necessary to make art beautiful. "But my time . . ." I said. He interrupted me: "The lesson! The lesson!" And so for a long hour the neighbors were treated to that special noise of someone practicing and repeating as their teacher looks on.

When the hour came to an end and the labors were over and peace restored, I demanded my due. If Signore F. was satisfied with his students, he would play whatever piece they requested. The reward I requested that day was a piece of Russian music that he had played the previous day.

* * *

An Arabian Mosaic

He sat at the piano, and before he started playing, we talked about the concert and exchanged views about the voices of the male and female singers, eventually arriving at *that story*. I asked him: "Is she one of your students?"

"No, no. She's one of Lady K.'s students. She's been to her house several times."

"Sometimes they call her Madame and sometimes Mademoiselle. Is she married or single?"

He sighed and said: "Poor woman!"

"What's so terrible about her life that it makes you feel so sorry for her?"

"Who wouldn't feel sorry for a woman who has beauty, intelligence, and goodness, who's been given everything she needs to be happy, and yet has had nothing but misery in life?"

"What misery?"

"What? Don't you know her story?"

"I know little bits here and there. You can't really get a clear picture of someone's life from what people say."

He sighed again, and then his fingertips hurried over the musical scale, as if he were releasing some of his grief, or looking for a new way to tell an old story. Then his expression clouded and he said: "Her father was a judge in the mixed courts.[1] He was very knowledgeable and intelligent, so he taught his daughter and gave her the best education. When the time came for her to be married the same thing happened to her as happens to a lot of girls. Her parents chose a fiancé for her, a foreigner, and she had no say about him. The fiancé was

---

[1] A system of civil courts in Egypt, presided over by Egyptian and foreign judges, with jurisdiction over residents of foreign nationalities. They operated from 1876 to 1949.

The Lady with the Story

rather handsome, so she didn't object. She was content, as many of her sisters are content, to have the usual clothes and bracelets and freedom. So she got married and had a magnificent wedding, to which the most prominent people from the local European colonies were invited. It wasn't long before the husband claimed what had been agreed as a dowry."

The professor stopped talking. A look of combined shame, compassion, and contempt came over his face. After a moment of silence he said: "Many women make men unhappy. Many women tear marriages apart and break people's hearts. But if a woman's not a wicked person, then she's really unfortunate. However much she rises up in her own eyes, however much she's liberated from her chains, and however much those who defend her rights exaggerate in raising her to a man's level, her life, her entire life, remains in the grip of this being—this man—whose equal she claims to be. In reality, she's nothing but what he wants her to be. If he's free and noble, he makes her free and noble. If he's low and mean, he debases and humiliates her. She's his plaything; she's his slave; something he need show no restraint with, whatever the situation. Men who have a conscience are frightened by this authority over woman, and this power. It's a power that scoffs at changes in politics and society, because it's stronger than either of them, and more firmly rooted—in nature itself. So they refrain from marrying out of fear of themselves."

His comments were important, but they irritated me—I wanted to hear the rest of the story. So I said: "Then what happened?"

"What happened is that this imposter had a secret

relationship with another woman and needed money, and marriage was the easiest way to get it. After three weeks, he disappeared."

"How did he disappear?"

"He left the house and never came back. For the first few days, his wife went mad, thinking he had died. Weeks went by and the news that he had gone off with his first wife started to spread. So they sent people out to look for him in his own country, Italy," and here Signore F. swallowed hard because he was Italian, "but the efforts of the police were in vain. They found no trace of him, either in Italy or in any other country in the West. Not long after this, the woman's father died—the woman who'd been cheated out of her youth, love, money, and standing. She became lonely and poor. The church refused to annul her marriage because the man hadn't married his first wife in church; it was a marriage by agreement only. There's a legal penalty for this, but how can the law reach someone who's vanished? Even if the church annulled the woman's marriage, people would still have their suspicions about her, because the one who's wronged is more exposed to suspicions and speculations than the wrongdoer. Especially if the wronged person is a woman and the wrongdoer is a man. That's why people watch every move she makes. She's settled on their tongues and become a tasty morsel for their chitchat. Even if she were to spend her days fasting, praying, and living the life of an ascetic, they wouldn't give her her due. No matter how high a price she paid them, they wouldn't sell her that illusory regard with which they flatter people of power and wealth and authority, or those who are good at duping them. What

The Lady with the Story

purpose does this woman have in life? She's not divorced, so she isn't free to spend her time as she wants; and she isn't chained, so she can't console herself by breaking her chains. It's a crippled sort of life. Man made her miserable, just as man has crippled many other women before her and made them miserable."

"But how is it she herself didn't feel during the engagement period that he was deceiving her?"

"I don't know how she didn't realize. And her family didn't notice anything either."

"Perhaps he was sincere when he married her, but kept thinking of the other woman. Perhaps she was very beautiful."

"Those who know her say she's an old gray-haired woman and are amazed that this bright, elegant man should be content with her—even as a servant." Signore F. lowered his head and remained silent for a while. Then he said: "But youth and beauty don't have any bearing on these things. People look for beauty in the salon, the theater, in society, and on the street, and the pretty woman usually attracts more attention than the not-so-pretty woman. But her effect doesn't go beyond this—history proves my point. The most recent historical example is that of the crown prince of Austria, whose murder set off World War I. He was the one who turned away from all the Austrian archduchesses and their dazzling beauty, and turned away from all the princesses in the ruling dynasties, and abdicated from the throne and the crown to marry a woman who was the least graceful and beautiful of all. That was the Countess Sophia Chotek, a lady-in-waiting to one of his female relatives. After

An Arabian Mosaic

her marriage she became the Duchess of Hohenberg, and was killed with him in the tragic incident at Sarajevo."

Signore F. settled himself in his seat and began to play a sad, stirring piece by Beethoven: the Requiem for a Hero.

* * *

Yesterday in a garden on the outskirts of Cairo I saw the lady with the story. I understand now why the expression in her eyes changes, and if I don't yet fully realize what the words "crippled life" mean, I do realize that life prepares circumstances for some people that they never dream of, and if they were to dream of them, they would try to eliminate them, even if it meant walking on thorns and burning coal. I have learned that in that straight figure, in that body which expresses strength and pride, there is a heart once wounded by true love. But today it is tortured by a cancer whose roots are spreading to all its corners, that deep-seated cancer which cannot be extracted: contempt for life and lack of trust in people.

I Want Him a Free Man

Layla Bin Mami

I'M IN A STRANGE STATE TONIGHT, STRANGE, STRANGE. I used to live in a whirlwind of thoughts, opinions, and principles, which removed me from the reality of life, from its original course, carrying me off suddenly toward what was outside the realms of life, what was far away from it, and from its reality!

My hand was a part of me. I'd forgotten all about it until . . . one day I became aware of its existence again. Its functions multiplied, so I restricted it to a few of them, and refused the hand its freedom. I didn't respond to its rebellion—I, a woman who wants everything to respond to her rebellion. The hand was a part of me. It was demanding, together with my other parts, the ultimate rebellion that I myself was seeking. But it wanted to have a rebellion of its own, alone; it was demanding a rebellion from me—me, an integrated whole, with the exception of my hand! Why? I don't know! I refused the hand its freedom. I believed in the freedom of the individual, but I forgot the freedom of the part. I neglected it. My mistake was . . . to neglect it.

I neglected my hand, a piece of me, an inseparable part. But I was neglected too. I needed a man confronting me who would make me feel the need for inner rebellion, for external rebellion. But my hand, it too needed to be confronted with another hand, to arouse it to rebel. And it rebelled against *me*. Wasn't I a believer in freedom? I was . . . pieces . . . parts, scattered abroad in the distant past, and coming together to form *me*. The hand knew how it worked together with its sisters—the small parts—to ignite a rebellion in my soul. And today it wanted to conduct its own rebellion, alone, without asking its sisters for help, so that its rebellion would be against me, and against what was outside both of us. It was rebelling for itself. By itself. Against me. Because I taught it to rebel. Or rather, it learned to rebel by itself . . .

What did the hand want? It answered: "Something simple. My ideal is part of your ideal! You wanted your freedom in order to subdue another man. I want my freedom in order to subdue another hand!"

I asked myself just how much my freedom had helped me in subduing the other man. The answer came to me. I knew now. I had subdued the other man by raising my word when he raised his, by expressing my opinion when he expressed his, by making choices when he made his, by becoming as indispensable as he was. I had subdued him, and we lived as I wanted, and as he wanted. But today my hand was agitating me. It wanted to rebel against me, to subdue the other hand. I hadn't yet distinguished the signs of its rebellion when it occurred. The hand broke its prison chains and set itself free, looking for the other hand in order to subdue it. Its fingertips spread out toward the fingertips of the other hand, responding—I wouldn't know how—to thousands of calls. Calls I was unaware of. My hand was becoming free, living, and I had only got as far as asking what the benefits of its liberation would be. It was living, and I

I Want Him a Free Man

had only got as far as asking what the benefits of its rebellion would be. My own rebellion hadn't been destructive. It had enabled me to subdue the other man.

And what of the hand's rebellion? I didn't know. What was its purpose? What would it accomplish? I hesitated between waiting and surrendering to the urge to forget it. Waiting was something I wasn't used to. I lived. The minutes alone passed—they had to. I didn't wait for them. I didn't wait for what they might bring. I let them pass. They passed because . . . they had to. I didn't want to wait because . . . I didn't have to. I surrendered to the urge to forget the hand, but I couldn't. Even though I no longer felt it, I saw it, I noticed it. It had disengaged itself from my feeling, but it hadn't disengaged itself from my mind. I had neglected it. My senses had lost track of it; but the fragments of its attributes had remained in my memory, in my mind. I saw the hand's movements, and I waited. No, I wasn't waiting. I was paying heed, until the moment the hand achieved a result. Until it became what it wanted—what that was, I didn't know—or until it failed to become what it wanted. It was enough that it had rebelled; it had felt its existence, and wanted it. It didn't matter *what* it would achieve, because it was bound to achieve something. The hand said it had adopted my ideal. It, a part of the whole, had adopted a lesser ideal from the great ideal. The ideal that I had formulated, with its help. It was a part of my parts. It was *my* part of the parts, the only one able to formulate an ideal. It formulated it by itself, because it had learned what power was. It knew how to derive benefit from what was around it. Its experiences were parts of my experiences. Its participation in my experiences, its partial participation, taught it the entire experience. And it set itself free, to experiment . . .

I was amazed. Had the other hand—the thought startled me—had the other hand set itself free from its master or had it merely surrendered to him? It ought to be clear that what my hand did wasn't in surrender to my will, my own will . . . I didn't want what it was doing!

I had wanted to become free, and I had gathered the small components of me, my parts, my limbs, and turned them into a great power, with which I demanded my freedom. I led them in the quest to obtain my freedom. And then I obtained it, and subdued you, the other man.

And here was my hand, assuming my character, and rebelling in its turn. It wanted its freedom. It, the little part, the part of my parts, wanted its freedom. Then it demanded it, and took it without my being able to prevent it.

And now it was practicing its freedom with your hand, which I regarded merely as submitting to your giant will, your deadly will.

You are a man: you didn't obtain your freedom alone; you didn't defend yourself for its sake; you didn't rebel against a condition which deprived you of it. You are a man born free. Yes, they granted you your freedom. They gave it to you as a gift, because you were incapable of demanding it. They knew you. They had tested your ability before, and your hand came out bearing your stamp. It wanted to be granted everything. It expected to be given something. It submitted to you, to your will, which you were granted at no cost.

As for my hand, it was like me. It didn't want to be

I Want Him a Free Man

offered cold food, free of charge. It wanted to struggle to obtain, in order to feel the pleasure of obtaining.

So he rebelled. And a failing pride rebelled in him. It made him lose the dearest thing he had. He pulled his hand from my hand. He set it free in a rebellion, a negative rebellion, which made him lose the hand he loved.

He retreated somewhere or other, urged on by a negative rebellion, pushed into it by a stupid pride. He wanted to be liberated from the love of freedom. He went away because he didn't understand. Why? I wanted to arouse him to rebel. He, who had always lived under the nightmare of submission, regarded me . . . as crazy. I disengaged my hand from myself. I gave it its freedom. I deemed myself above blind selfishness. And so I set my parts free. My hand became free, in order to lead its life unrestrained, in order to subdue the other hand.

And his hand became free, in order to lead its life under the nightmare of submission, in order that he should subdue it. He was a man subdued by society, subdued by life, and then he subdued his hand. Whereas I was a person who subdued society, who subdued life, and then my hand subdued me.

He refused life, refused freedom. And I preferred them to him, and left him forever, left him to live in the nightmare of submission. I couldn't tolerate his stupid pride, his empty pride.

Where To?

Kulit Suhayl al-Khuri

The isolated stella[1] gazes at the star and sparkles. Doesn't he realize that she's closer to him than he is to himself? Doesn't he feel that the light of her love defies the great studded distance between them, and fills it?

"Why don't we meet?"

The question is absorbed by the rays of the tender star.

"Why don't we meet?"

The call is drowned in her tears.

Her constant reply is a sparkle. How can she tell him that she fears for him because of her love? How can she explain to him that they have to fly above the stars and leave the sky altogether if they are to meet? The sky! She didn't ask to be a diamond in the nocturnal darkness, and the fact that she is a source of light doesn't dazzle her. She hates the sky. She hates the frost of the sky. But she won't wrest her beloved from his luminous world. It was decreed that they should be separated in the sky. For his sake, she will yield to the sky's will.

"Why don't we meet?"

---

[1]Stella is a Latin word meaning "female star." It was adopted here for lack of English equivalent for Arabic "najma."

Her pride forbids her to reveal her true feelings. She twinkles ironically:

"We were created to adorn the sky!"

The star shines vigorously, ecstatically:

"And to illuminate the earth!"

The rays draw blood from her wound and pour down onto the earth.

There, on the seashore, two people are walking side by side, their hands clasped together. They sit on a rock, clinging to each other.

The tender stella twinkles, and her wounded twinkle excites the star.

"They're human beings," she says. "But we, we live in the heights and can't do what earthly people do."

He lights up: "We can if we want. If we want."

The stella wanes, frightened. Does he know the price? The stars must pay for happiness. And the price of their meeting is very high. She suppresses her yearning:

"But we don't want to. Our duty in life is loftier than we can pretend to forget. Ordinary men need you to stay in the heights. Passers-by need your light."

Sparks of scorn fly from the star:

"We stars delude ourselves that ordinary men need us. It's an illusion with which we console ourselves. An illusion in whose mirage-like warmth we hide in order to forget the frost of our existence."

The stella calms down, agreeing:

"Yes, we give, and passers-by don't understand the meaning of giving."

Where To?

The two passers-by on the shore are drinking in the dual agonies exploding in rays above them. The youth raises his head to the sky and addresses the girl:

"Look how wonderful our stars are, and how pure our sky is!"

Lost in thought, the girl murmurs:

"How narrow the earth is! I wish we lived in the vastness of the sky! I wish we were two everlasting stars!"

The youth contemplates her admiringly, his gaze lost in hers. He puts his arm around her shoulders, whispering: "I love you!"

The stella glitters and the star flares up:

"Love, love. A word ordinary men constantly repeat without understanding the meaning of it."

He turns toward the stella and glares out his confession:

"I love you. I love you the way no human being can love. I love you with my fire and my light. I love you with every heavenly treasure and gift there is in my existence."

The stella trembles in tears, and her glow increases. Will she tell him that her only wish is to fly to him? No!

Her grief pours down in blazing strands, enveloping the two wide-awake people on the shore.

The girl leans her head on the youth's warm shoulder and asks teasingly:

"How much do you love me?"

The youth embraces her:

"So much that I'll give you everything I own. I want to marry you!"

The star flashes: "How stupid earthly people are!" Suddenly he blinks in alarm. How much does his stella love him? His hopeful gleam engulfs the stella, and she shines:

"I love you . . . I love you even to the point of giving up my place in the eternal frost so that you can stay in the sky!"

The star shudders, amazed, and sprinkles the shore with silver. Who told her that he wants to stay in the sky? Should he confess to her that without her his luminous world makes him miserable, because he lives in it with a dead heart? He darkens:

"How miserable it makes me!"

The stella turns pale. What point is there in her sacrifice if it doesn't rescue him from his misery? What sense is there in her pride when it makes her a coward? Her misgivings ebb away. Why not turn his constant misery and her unending unhappiness into a moment of joy? She lights up:

"Won't you be sorry to leave the sky?"

He gleams: "The moment of our meeting will be greater than the sky!"

"Why don't we meet then?"

The question makes her tearful.

"Why don't we meet?"

The call has now become part of her.

The star sparkles in fear. Does he have the right to stand in the way of her eternity? As long as he is far away from her, she is eternal. Their being together means conflagration!

"We shall burn up!"

Intoxicated, she suggests:

"What point is there in my eternity if I live in deprivation?" Then she opens up her arms, determined:

"The moment of our being together will live forever! At that moment I will discharge my light. It doesn't matter to me that afterward I'll be extinguished!"

The star's longing is rekindled, and he trembles with happiness.

"Let's leave the sky!"

She flies above the stars.

"Let's meet!"

They meet.

"Let's burn up!"

On the shore the girl sighs deeply and the youth asks:

"What's the matter?"

"Nothing. I saw a shooting star!"

"It's a wishing star! Did you make a wish?"

She laughs shyly:

"Yes."

He embraces her and tenderly asks:

"What did you wish?"

"I wished . . . I wished our love would shine and last forever like the stars!"

The Cat

Layla Baalbakki

We are now at the beginning of summer. In February, the cat gave birth to her little kittens on a small road where the municipal workmen were laying asphalt and had thrown away their leftovers and dirty handkerchiefs. The mother spent the first days licking the blood from the little bodies. One night, when the rain was beating down mercilessly in the street, and the cold was creeping into the mother's limbs and the little kittens' paws, and the thunder was drowning every voice on earth, and the lightning was slashing the face of the sky—on this particular night the kittens' mother heard soft footfalls on the paving stones outside the iron barrel, and they startled her. She pulled her kittens closer and rubbed their bodies to warm them up. Then she slowly sniffed them. The soft footfalls were hovering, hovering. The kittens' mother knew them. She had heard them at the window of the house where she used to live, and her heart trembled. That was months ago, when she lived with two old people, their only bachelor son, and the maid. Everybody spoiled her and was proud of her. She had the most beautiful eyes, sometimes violet, sometimes grayish-blue. She was slender, and her white fur, spotted with honey-colored circles, shone like a mirror reflecting the rising sun. She lived like a princess, sharing in the household's simple, quiet, and pleasant life. "What shall we cook today, Jasmine?" "The old man's smoking a lot, Jasmine." "The boy's late, Jasmine." "Jasmine."

The mistress had explained to her that her name meant a white flower that lives only for a short time and then disappears. Its smell, she said, was the strongest, softest, and best of all flower perfumes. Why hadn't the mistress told her she resembled the jasmine flower only in its fleeting life, which faded like stars on a bright night? Anyway, what mattered was that she had seen his stubborn, giant figure filling the window. She had stolen glances at him, and whispered to herself that he was the most beautiful cat she had ever seen, that she felt weak and numb when she saw him, and that love with him would be wonderful. So she left the house one evening, followed him in his meanderings, and gave him love. Lots and lots of love. He drenched her with love, buried her with love, choked her with love. She was the richest cat in the world. This, at least, is what she felt, as she responded to the feelings, the colors, the pulse of those moments loaded with pleasure and trembling and fear. And he, this cat who was hovering round the barrel now, he gave her more than love: he gave her the babies. And she, because of the babies, would continue to respond to him, to follow him, to dream of him.

The soft footfalls of the kittens' father died away, and the storm intensified. The kittens' mother listened, alert. The little kittens looked up at their mother's face, questioning, and the mother reassured them that all was safe again in their refuge, and that they would find another hideout the next day.

The Cat

When the storm abated and dawn broke, the kittens' mother began to move her little babies. She thought it best to scatter them in different places, and so it was that one of them ended up in a lighted kitchen window.

The little cat didn't know what had happened to her mother and sisters. All she knew was that there was a smell of milk escaping from the open window, and she stretched her head toward it. A fat woman spotted her. She dragged her in savagely, threw her on the floor, and said in a mean and raucous voice: "This cat's arrived at the right time. She's going to clear the house of mice, and she'll get nothing to eat except what she catches!" To begin with, the mice didn't come out of their nests. Even if they had, the cat wouldn't have recognized them, because she had never encountered a mouse before. As a result, she was forced to steal a lot of milk in order not to die of hunger before the encounter with the mice took place. One night she was dozing off in the darkness on a chair in the corner of the kitchen, when she heard a light, unusual movement. She opened one eye and saw a group of mice, big ones and small ones—perhaps a whole family. She got ready to challenge them. Then she closed her eyes and felt fear and disgust at the mere thought of one day being forced to eat these revolting creatures. She asked herself how she could possibly swallow a creature that size. Why, anyway, did she have to treat them as enemies? Who knows, perhaps they were kinder than the fat woman. She jumped down from the chair onto the tiled floor to welcome the guests, but they dispersed, startled. She looked around and on one of the shelves she saw a sack overflowing with flour, then she understood. She stole away into the living room, clearing the mice's way for a safe assault.

In the morning the fat woman discovered the conspiracy, and she beat the cat and threw her out. After that, the cat wandered in and out of many houses, where she was beaten, imprisoned, starved, and forced to kill even large rats and worms and gnats . . . Finally, she discovered a neglected garden and settled there, eating whatever the wealthy and wasteful dropped from their balconies, and roaming inside her plot of land, singing and rejoicing. Now she was on her own territory, free and nameless.

As for me, when my mother was pregnant with me, she was in love with someone other than my father. Because she loved this person so intensely, I turned out very, very pretty, and everyone who sees me just keeps saying: "She's so pretty. She's so pretty." I'm now nineteen years old. I'm determined not to become pregnant unless I'm drowning in a stormy sea of love. Then the face of my child will look out onto the world like the rising moon. The moon? No. The moon is cold, stupid. It has no meaning. No. The face of my child will look out like the radiant sun. Had I lived in the age of paganism, I would be one of the sun's slave girls, worshipping it in the temple and burning incense. And the earth. This is the first time I've thought of the earth. The earth doesn't interest me: the soil, the trees, the rocks, the springs. What interests me is to be dearly loved on this earth. And now I have a man who loves me. This is the only thing that gives me satisfaction.

I know what I want. Meanwhile, my feet sink into the earth and my face embraces the sun in anticipation that

The Cat

someone will reach the moon to wipe it out and relieve me of its stupid light. I know that I won't struggle to be a free woman and a heroine and immortal. It gives me pleasure to be going to university this year, and to share in the clamor, boredom, superficiality, and sweet dreams of my family, and in the depravity of some of its members, and their cowardice. I get lost at home, and I dissolve in the street, and with this I feel that I'm safe, and I dream calmly, calmly, and with pleasure.

No. I'm not like those legendary women who are able to live alone. Loneliness? It kills me. Places empty of human beings frighten me. That's why I intend to get married and have a lot of children. In the meantime, I'm unable, unable to breathe, if there isn't a man at my side who loves me. As for myself, I haven't been in love yet.

This person sitting next to me in the car, listening carefully and alertly to the mewing of the cat, he's the man with whom I roam the city these days. Although his age is twice my own nineteen years, he is happier than I am. He's the one who taught me to laugh, and the one who discovered that my laughter betrays longing, that my smile is the blossoming of a tulip, that my complexion is the red, velvety petals of a rose, and that my eyes are a harbor guiding sailors to the shores of pleasure, to the prize diamond, to victory.

What I like about him is the gray hair on his temples. It's the only thing that makes my fingers go numb. Once he asked me what I wanted from him, and I said: "Your gray hair." His eyes grew pensive, and his cheeks paled. Then he pulled me toward him and showered me with kisses. He didn't leave one atom of my body unkissed. When he kisses me, I feel as if I'm bathing in a rivulet under a walnut tree, while far away on the rugged road a villager carries a load of wheat to the mill. And the mill is on top of the mountain.

I made him understand from the start that I know what I want, and that I don't intend to fall madly in love with him and abandon my world to dart off on horseback after him to some unknown forest. That's why we've never talked about his wife or his house or his work. And I haven't told him anything about my life. We go out to dinner, we dance, we swim, we climb mountains. I'm his spring, and he's my summer. We have fun.

But he surprises me.

He surprised me just now in the car. Instead of putting his arm round my shoulder and letting my head rest in the hollow between his chin and shoulder, then moistening my eyes, my mouth, and my neck with his tongue; instead of driving the car wildly with one hand through the city streets, he sat stiffly, his eyes exploring the courtyard of the club and the neglected garden. "Can you hear a cat mewing?" he asked. "Yes, I can," I answered. He jumped out and ordered: "Go on slowly. I'll pick up the cat and take her to my father so he can play with her." He disappeared behind a hedge of bright flowers for a short time and then emerged, clutching a skinny little cat that was rending the air with her mewing. He threw the cat onto the back seat, rolled up the window, then drove like a maniac through the streets. I shut my eyes, afraid that any minute he would crash into a wall or knock someone over. I hadn't seen him so proud, triumphant, and happy, as he was just then. Without turning to me he said: "I'm going back to give the cat to my father to play with. After that we'll have

The Cat

dinner." And then I felt lonely, so lonely, and sad; I almost suffocated; I longed to cry but didn't open my mouth. I gave vent to my emotions in one sudden, magic act: I stretched out my hand in the darkness of the car to the back seat. The cat had calmed down and stopped mewing, and I couldn't make her out behind me. I ran my fingers over the rough carpet, at the same time scrutinizing my man's face out of the corner of my eye. He was ecstatic, his glance wandering beyond the houses and the lights and the people on the street. I opened the window on my side, and began again to search the carpet with my other hand. As if anticipating her salvation, the cat drew near my fingers. I seized her, then squeezed her soft body with my fingers. This time she screamed. I pulled my hand back and began to tremble. I breathed in relief when he didn't turn around but said: "My father will be so happy with the cat. He'll have fun with her." I smiled secretly in exhaustion. I shut my eyes, put my hand on her belly, lifted her up carefully, and threw her out of the window into the street. Then I hurriedly rolled up the window and passed a cold hand across my flushed face. I didn't dare look at his face after that. My hair was getting in my eyes, and I wished it were as long as palm leaves, so I could hide myself behind it. I struggled for words. "Drop me off at a café," I said. Judging by his voice, he wasn't surprised: "We'll have dinner on the mountain, as agreed," he said, "after I've taken the cat to my father to play with." But I shouted: "Drop me off at a café!" The pain was creeping further into my hand, my chest was getting tighter, and the sadness was paralyzing my feet.

"Drop me off here!"

An Arabian Mosaic

He stopped the car in front of the café, saying: "What's the matter? Wait here till I've delivered the cat."

I dragged my feet to the door but I didn't go in. Instead, I hurried away to wander in the silent, deserted alleyways.

The Cat, the Maid, and the Wife

DAISY AL-AMIR

HER VISIT TO HER FRIEND WAS DELAYED FOR MONTHS. The friend begged her to come, and she promised to look her up when she had time.

The friend had time for visits, but she had to work. How could her friend understand that what prevented her coming was the fact that she had so much work? How could someone who didn't know how to pass her time understand that someone else's time was completely taken up?

But the friend's pleas and continuous insistence on the need to see her embarrassed her. So that day she put off some work, knowing that the next day would be fuller as a result.

There was no one else at her friend's house. The children were at school, or so she thought, until their mother said she had tired of them and sent them to her mother-in-law so that she could have a rest from them.

"A rest from them? But they're your children!"

"I'm tired of everything."

"You've got a diploma in psychology. Why don't you bring them up properly, so they don't upset you or annoy you?"

An Arabian Mosaic

The friend laughed tearfully:

"Do you think it's only up to me to bring them up? What shall I tell their father? And their grandmother? What shall I tell all the members of my family, and their father's family? Every one of them has a say in their upbringing!"

The friend carried on talking quite freely, surprising her by saying:

"I hate my husband. I despise him."

This remark astonished her. A wife who hates her husband yet continues to live with him? But before she could make any comment, the wife continued:

"My husband respects me because I'm the daughter of a minister. He hopes this will get him to be appointed director-general. I myself don't actually respect my father. I have a very low opinion of all the people who praise him, because I know as well as they do that he's a thief!"

The maid came in, carrying two cups of coffee. The mistress of the house stopped talking, and she remained silent until the maid had left.

"Do you smoke?" asked the minister's daughter, and then went on quite freely: "I smoke a lot. It's a release for me, but I do it when my husband's not there. He doesn't like women to smoke." She lit the two cigarettes. "I once saw you in a public place take a pack of cigarettes out of your purse, light one, and smoke it at your ease. I envied you. Aren't you afraid of what people might say?"

She wanted to answer, but her friend interrupted her:

"My husband indulges in all the vices. So do all the men in the family, depending on their particular tastes.

The Cat, the Maid, and the Wife

I've been waiting to see you for some time. Twice I was told you had gone on a trip, once for business and once for pleasure. Which one of your trips did you enjoy more?"

"The trip home to my own country . . ."

Her friend interrupted her:

"Home . . . home . . . Do you feel you have a home country? Do you know your home country? I . . . I . . . I'd like to know where *my* home country is, so I could go there. I hope it does you good. Are you happy when you talk about your home country? What's happiness anyway? How can one feel happy talking about a home country? I feel a dreadful darkness around me. We all exploit each other. Our family is a group of enemies. I'm tired of all the hatred. I want to love, to be allowed to love . . . I want love . . . I want to . . ."

The maid came in and the mistress of the house stopped talking and remained silent until the maid had left with the two cups of coffee.

"I'm worried . . . I'm worried the maid has concluded from what I was saying that I want *someone* to love . . . Maybe she'll think I love someone other than my husband . . . I'm worried she'll assume I want to cheat on my husband, or that I'm already cheating on him. She doesn't know I'm cheating myself by living with him when I hate him. As for him . . . if he could cheat on me, if he could manage not to be afraid of my father, the minister, he'd cheat on me with the maid. I'd like to announce what I think of my father in the newspapers, to see what my husband would do then . . ."

This time the guest interrupted her:

"Will you go on living like this?"

"What can I do? Commit suicide? I wish I could write a letter and say everything in it, everything. A letter that would be published in the newspapers, so that the people would know. But who would publish a letter like that? They're afraid of my father, the minister. My husband, the minister's son-in-law, would burn it. My husband's family would spread rumors that I was an evil woman, that I had tried to hide my evil nature, and that *that* was why I had committed suicide. My family . . . they would get a doctor's certificate to show I had died a natural death. They'd even stop me enjoying death! But what about me? I don't live a natural life, so don't I have the right to refuse to live? Don't I have the right to let people know this?

"Suicide isn't the only way. There are a thousand other ways to express refusal. Try to reveal your rejection of this kind of life through other means. For example . . ."

Suddenly the husband came in. He rushed over to greet the friend and say how proud he was to see her and salute the struggling working woman. He regarded her as an exemplary woman, because she had been assertive and established herself. The friend interrupted him:

"I wonder if you truly are proud of women like me. Do you really mean it? Would you like your wife to be like me?"

"My wife . . . my wife's a different sort of person. She's supported and protected. Her father's a minister, her husband's . . ." he laughed loudly, "a director-general. She has a well-established family around her. Why would she need to work and struggle?"

She looked at the wife. She stared at her, silently

The Cat, the Maid, and the Wife

urging her to say something, to make some sort of declaration, just to utter one word. She waited. The silence continued. She offered the wife a cigarette. She refused it, saying she didn't smoke.

The husband settled into his chair then called the maid and asked her to make him a cup of coffee. The wife jumped up from her seat mechanically and cried:

"I'll make it myself. You like the coffee I make myself!"

When the room was empty except for the husband and herself, the guest got up and walked to the door. She had no intention of saying goodbye to the mistress of the house, making coffee herself for a husband she despised.

Back in the kitchen of her own house she found several bundles of clothes. Her maid, dressed in her best clothes, was sitting on a chair, waiting. She looked around, unable to understand.

"I'm leaving, madam," said the maid.

"Leaving? Without a reason? What's happened?"

"My honor's the most important thing to me," said the maid.

She didn't understand this answer.

"But who's offended your honor?"

"Your husband. He asked me for his telephone book. When I told him I didn't know where he'd put it, he screamed at me, saying over and over again that I was to get it, even if I had to dig it out of the ground. He accused me of lying and stealing. I'm not his wife. He shouldn't be taking it out on me like that."

"But where will you go? It's almost ten o'clock at night and you're a stranger in this city!"

"There are plenty of hotels, and I'll contact my children. There are men in my family who can protect me."

She didn't say to her: "Then why are you working as a maid when you're so old? Why aren't your children supporting you?" All the events of the day were jumbled in her head. She didn't know where to start.

The packages and bundles of clothes were moved out of the house. She heard the sound of the door closing behind the maid, but she stood there, undecided. Should she admire the maid or be angry with her? Should she go after her or respect her decision?

When she finally went down the stairs and reached the street, the maid had already disappeared into the long dark street. She stood there, contemplating her surroundings, overwhelmed by the whirl of events.

A cat walked past her. It stopped to scrutinize the lady standing in the dark street, then it carried on, its long tail hanging, relaxed, behind it.

It was a dirty, skinny cat, and obviously hungry. She called it: "Pst, pst." But it didn't turn round. It crossed the street and jumped over the broken wall around the vacant lot.

There was no sound of a male cat calling its mate in the vacant lot, surrounded by a broken wall. And the lonely, dirty, hungry cat wasn't mewing either.

A Woman Worth Less than Nothing
Hayat Ibn al-Shaykh

When he saw me the first time, he looked at me with admiration and said I was pretty, sweet. When he spoke with me, he said I was enticing, wonderful. When he tried to put his hand on my shoulder to kiss me, he said I was complicated, because I pushed his hand away and refused his kiss. And when he invited me to his apartment and I said no, he said I was abnormal. So I left him, with his insults ringing in my ears: "Crazy girl . . . conceited." I rushed off in search of a drink and a cigarette. I wanted to blot out my frustration, and downfall, and the bewildering questions, swirling in my mind.

As I began to drink from the first glass, I said to myself perhaps I was really abnormal. Why was I abnormal? I wasn't sure. Perhaps because I didn't want anyone else but you, because I couldn't forget you. By the second glass, I felt I wasn't abnormal, just rather unruly, like a wild tigress that needs to indulge in physical activity. By the third glass, I realized I was an exemplary woman, a wonderful woman. How was I wonderful? Never mind . . . but I *was* wonderful, and the men I knew were all stupid, fatuous. They didn't understand me. I laughed

An Arabian Mosaic

. . . I wasn't laughing because they were stupid and fatuous; I had always known that. I was laughing because I was sure I was truly wonderful . . . perhaps. By the fourth glass, the thoughts began to battle in my head; obvious truths began to crowd in front of my eyes. I tried to shut my eyes in order not to see the red warning light flashing in front of them. I was in the process of discovering something else: I wasn't wonderful, I wasn't exemplary; I was a stupid, failed woman . . . a desperate woman. I didn't know how to live or what to do. I was heading for madness, that was all. This was the plain truth I had pretended not to see for years and years. Only now did it finally dawn on me. By the fifth glass, I had become convinced that I was nothing, that I couldn't possibly amount to anything as long as I loved you, because my love for you choked everything reasonable in my life, and my desire for you put a slur on my name and what was best in my life. I smashed the glass and dragged my feet to the darkness of my house, weeping for my failed life, the life I had discovered was nothing. In the alleyways . . . on the walls . . . on the quilt and pillow, I could see words written in a red as dark as the blood coagulating on the chest of a slaughtered bird: *a woman worth less than nothing.*

I couldn't bear the effect of these words for long, so I threw the pillow and the quilt and the papers and the books on the floor and trampled on them. Then I went in search of a drink that would tell me I was a wonderful woman, not abnormal or stupid. But I found nothing. The words, dark red like the blood coagulating on the chest of a slaughtered bird, were dancing in front of me. I saw them in every corner of the house: *a woman worth*

A Woman Worth Less than Nothing

less than nothing . . . So I hurried away, running from the hateful words, from the constant buzzing that split my head.

I began to walk about in the empty streets, chewing over my exasperation, shaking off my hesitation, gulping at the cups of my failure and despair. I looked at the sky. The bright moonlight filled my eyes. I stood still, gazing at the moon and asking myself: "Why can't I have the moon? I want it. How can I reach it? Would I be able to reach it if I wanted to?" I began to laugh, convinced that I was stupid, silly. What was there in the moon for me to desire? The moon sheds its light from far away, but in fact it is just a solid rock with nothing on it but frost. The frost I hate. It deceives us with its pure light. The vast distance disguises the truth about it. And so it attracts silly girls like me, who are fond of absurdity.

Once again I began to chew over my exasperation, to shake off my hesitation, and to gulp at the cups of my failure and despair. I remembered that when I was a naive little girl, I had wanted the sun. My mother used to hit me when she found me spending hours gazing at it, my eyes red from its rays, my body sweaty from its heat. My father constantly rebuked me, saying if I didn't stop looking at the sun, it would one day tumble down on my head, burn me up, and leave me a pile of bones. But I would laugh and make fun of what he said. I would go off resolutely to break up one of my mother's necklaces and throw the beads up one by one toward the sun, trying to hit it. I would carry on until I felt almost blinded by the burning rays, until my eyes were overflowing with tears, and the buzzing in my head grew louder and louder with the intense heat. The beads of the stolen necklace would be scattered here and there, having failed to hit their target. Then I would look at the sky and shout, cursing the sun and the moon and my thoughts, teetering on the edge of madness and absurdity.

I was sure now that I wanted you, no one else but you, no matter what had happened or what would happen. Through the veils of darkness your bright face appeared to me—charming, handsome, and sweet, just as I knew and loved it. I saw your eyes, constantly filled with wonder and amazement, and felt I could almost drown in their sea of honey. I also realized you were more beautiful and sweeter—and farther away—than the sun and the moon.

I knew I wanted you and no one else but you. And that because of that, I was stupid, silly. I could have been something remarkable if I hadn't loved you and hadn't wanted you. So I would carry on living as I did, following you like a faithful dog following its master. But I was also sure that you were stupid like me, weak and vain, unable to say openly what you wanted, because you didn't know what to do or what to look for. And perhaps because of that I worshiped you.

I went home, dragging my tired feet, running away from the sun and the moon and you. I was no longer afraid of reading the words, dark red like the blood coagulating on the chest of a slaughtered bird, inscribed in the alleyways, on the quilt, on the pillow . . . *a woman worth less than nothing*. We had become *two people worth less than nothing, you and me*. And I would never know which one of us pulled the other in that direction, you or me.

I made my way back, trying to draw your picture.

A Woman Worth Less than Nothing

How would you look, I wondered, if I drew your picture? I imagined you without a body, without a heart or face, just two beautiful eyes, a sea of honey in which I could drown the frustrations of my life and the confusion of my thoughts, a sea from which I would drink even the dregs, till the spring ran dry and . . .

But what if I drew you as a face without eyes? Like the moon without light, or the sky without a sun or a moon, or the spring without flowers; like a rose without dew, or a river without water; like the statue of a blind god standing high up on a distant hill, and I a little pebble rolling between your legs, tossed about by the hurricane winds, flung to and fro by them, darting about with the current. But I would always come back to throw myself under your feet, to kiss the dust on the soles of your feet.

I threw the paintbrush to the floor, tore up the paper, and flung myself onto the bed to try to sleep. I had realized that you were a sly, mean god, made of mud and clay, who didn't deserve at all to be worshiped; that the honey that filled your eyes was bitter, dripping with a poison that killed anyone who tried to get a taste of it; that I was stupid and stubborn for loving you; that the whole world was fatuous, hateful; that people were fools, silly, duped; that everyone had ten horns blazing with fire, and six eyes dripping poison, and three open mouths waiting to bite anyone who dared to approach.

People had repeatedly said that I was rash, that I didn't know how to live. My female friends said that I was conceited, hesitant, that I didn't know what I wanted. And men, observing me from a distance, said I was sweet, wonderful. But when they got close they said I was strange, abnormal. And you always said I was stubborn, crazy. I knew you were saying that because I loved you and wanted you. But I hadn't yet understood who I was. All I knew was that I was a failed woman, a desperate woman, *a woman worth less than nothing.* A woman who was looking for herself but hadn't yet found herself.

Perhaps I *would* find myself—if I could forget you someday. Perhaps?

Half a Woman
Sufi Abdallah

Her heart beat furiously and she felt a surge of joy that set her body quivering. Her eyes roamed over the scene around her. Could she notice anything? Could she sense the droves of people and the crush around her? No, not at all. As the car made its way through the streets, her longing was almost leaping out from her heart, pushing her forward, as if she felt the car was moving too slowly and she was struggling against a desire to jump out and run off . . . to where she would meet him!

She paid the driver and rushed to the elevator. She ran into the apartment—the door was ajar, as it always was when she came, because he knew her appointed time—and looked around for him. In an instant she was in his arms, and he was holding her tightly, and whispering ecstatically in her ear:

"My darling . . . My darling . . ."

Rubbing her cheeks against his chest, she began to whisper with the same yearning:

"Rushdi . . . Rushdi . . ."

They fell into the trance of the meeting. Each was totally absorbed in the other, and everything became still around them, except for the passionate sighs, like steam rising from a fire ablaze inside her. When they had calmed down a little, he pulled her by the hand to the sofa and put his arms tenderly around her, touching her, as though afraid that she would dissolve from between his arms, or that, after all the time he had missed her, and whispered secrets to her, and put his arms around her, he would discover she was a mirage. He stretched out his fingers gently and lifted her chin. Their eyes met. It was a passionate, love-crazed look. He cried out:

"What are we to do?"

Yes, what were they to do? How could they possibly go on living like this? How long could she hold out against the burning flame of this love? She wondered if she would manage to lead a double life. She wondered if she had the strength to carry on with this comedy her whole life. Today she would make the break between her past and her future! Today she would say her last word to him! Today she would bring down a thick curtain on ten years of her life, ten years in which she had been the model of a faithful wife and devoted mother ... until she had seen *him*.

How did he manage to deprive her of her mind, her heart, and her being, and turn all the values that formed the fabric of her life into nothing? How did he manage to stifle all her motherly feeling, making love of life and the self and the desire for freedom and pleasure sweep away everything else? Was this what people called the irresistible power of love? Then there was no hope for her, no hope for life. She wondered what fate was lurking in wait for her, and what had come over her that she could change into the opposite of what she was.

Had she had an unhappy life?

She didn't know. They had married her off at eighteen

Half a Woman

to a successful businessman of thirty-five, handsome, daunting, self-possessed. He respected her and treated her kindly. She hadn't felt any change in her life, except for the physical engagements that she experienced with her husband at appointed times, without finding a response or a meaning to them. She had grown up in a small house as a member of a large family; now she was the mistress of a great villa. Her husband's behavior was steady; the times at which he slept, woke, sat, stood, and ate never varied. She never heard an improper word from him; his actions were marked by kindness, gentleness, companionship, and calmness. She had lived with him for ten years, and in that time had borne him Samih and Najwa, a boy and a girl, the delight of her eye and the focal point of her life. She was the exemplary wife of the successful businessman, slim, calmly beautiful, and self-assured. Her movements, her gestures were well considered. She lent grace and beauty to the parties given by her husband; she was an excellent housekeeper, a model mother, and an obedient wife, devoted to her good husband.

Her life flowed along in a single, unchanging mode, although in recent years the volume of her husband's work had grown, and the number of business trips he undertook at home and abroad had increased. His business had grown to such an extent that she rarely saw him. The children grew bigger and went to school. She had less say in their supervision, because care of them was entrusted to a German nanny born in Cairo. The nanny consistently refused to let anyone come between her and her children—as she called them—even if that person were their own mother, and even if seeing them gave their mother more joy and happiness than anything else on earth.

And suddenly Rushdi had burst into her life! She had seen him at a party where her husband was the center of attention. It wasn't the first time she had seen him. In fact, she had often seen him; he was a well-known personality in the world of literature and music. But she couldn't remember his ever having attracted her attention, or her ever having thought about him separately from the other people she had met. Even when she had greeted him, she had merely nodded from a distance. She couldn't remember ever having shaken his hand. So what on earth made it impossible, on that particular day, for her to take her eyes off him? What new feature in him had attracted her? And why had his eyes constantly searched her out, not letting her escape, as if he were trying to hypnotize her, plunging with her into the abyss, making her realize how heavy her body felt, how worn her nerves were, and how much she wanted to relax!

Things moved quickly after that day. They moved in a way that made her forget herself and her life and her husband and her children, until she no longer saw anyone but him. He had opened her eyes to the secret of life—a secret closed to every woman, so that she should discover it with her husband, the man who held sway over her life.

Rushdi was the man who had made her aware of her femininity, and then she had lost her balance and reason; she had surrendered control of her life to him.

What would happen to her husband if he lost her? He would be sad for a little while, then he would be whipped up into the whirlwind of work and forget her, like a

Half a Woman

phantom that had passed through his life and vanished. He wasn't even aware of her existence; she was like a piece of furniture that he was used to seeing in its usual place. If he found the place empty, he would feel a lump in his throat, but it wouldn't be long before he consigned her to oblivion . . . And what about her children? How could her heart ever agree to leave them? With whom would she leave them? In fact, they had grown up and didn't need her anymore, and there was someone there to look after them and to provide them with the necessities of life.

She wondered if she was deceiving herself. Was it possible for her children to replace her with that nanny? Had her affection so dried up that she thought the necessities of life were all that those two little darlings wanted in the way of care?

Maybe they would be sad when she left, but they would surely forget her: the hearts of children are easily impressed and quick to forget. It was better for her to leave a good memory of their life together in her children's hearts, before deprivation made her lose her equanimity and pour her hatred out over them—if she let Rushdi slip away from her.

In any event, she wouldn't be able to continue to live like this now that she had tasted the sweetness of love. And even if she wanted to, Rushdi wouldn't agree to it. He was mad about her. He presented her with a choice: either they ran away together and got married, once she had demanded a divorce from her husband, or else he would leave the country and wander about, because jealousy gnawed at his heart and tortured his soul when he pictured her with someone else. He wouldn't be happy until she had become his, heart and soul.

What should she do? She was caught between two fires—her children and her love! But would she be able to face life after him, if she let him go?

No, no, she couldn't face it. Nor could she lead a double life any longer. And if she didn't enjoy her life now, how miserable it would be then! She would be no more than the remains of a woman; every mouthful she ate, every garment she wore would be pathetic!

Yes, she would become the remains of a woman. Any woman who lost her heart and her nerves and her emotions was nothing but remains! A body without a soul, a corpse crawling but lifeless! That frightened her. The years she had already lost were enough for her to want to start all over, before she wasted the blossom of her youth and the fragrance of her life.

The children were asleep, and her husband was away on one of his trips. She told the nanny she would be away for three days at her aunt's in Tanta, and then she left, carrying a suitcase with some of her clothes in it. She urged the nanny to take good care of the two children until she came back.

She left in a hurry, as if someone were chasing her. She threw herself into the first cab she found and told the driver to hurry to the station in time for the eight o'clock evening train.

He had gone to Alexandria two days earlier to make preparations for a long stay. Although the hard thinking of those two days had exhausted her, she had become all the more convinced that she had no life without him and that it was futile to think of turning back. That time had confirmed to her beyond doubt that it was impossible to break the relationship—so let whatever was coming come!

The short hours of the journey seemed like an age. Her thoughts focused on a single unchanging point: the moment of meeting—although she couldn't prevent painful pricks of conscience from piercing her now and again, as she imagined the state of her children when they faced the new day without jumping onto her bed and delighting her with kisses and hugs and laughter.

Would they be sad? Would they suffer? How long would it be before they stopped missing her and forgot her?

The train stopped. The "yearning one" was waiting for her as usual, burning with longing and agony and passion. As soon as they were ensconced in his car and she was wrapped in his arms, she forgot the children, and the house, and the whole world.

They spent the night locked in each other's arms, as if time had stopped, as if the world would end within the hour.

As she dozed off, she was startled by a picture flashing across her mind. It was her daughter, Najwa, jumping onto her bed to give her the morning hug. But she couldn't respond, she was as stiff as death. She could see her and hear her, but she couldn't speak to her. The girl let out a resounding scream:

"Mama! Mama!"

Then she broke into a painful cry.

She opened her eyes, alarmed. She sat up in the bed and looked around, baffled. Where was she? Where did she belong?

An Arabian Mosaic

A thin thread of morning light penetrated the wooden shutter and slid into the middle of the room, which was drowned in darkness. She turned round, and there he was, snoring happily and contentedly, his lips parted in a soft smile.

The events of the previous day crowded into her mind. Without thinking about it, she got out of the bed, hurriedly took off her nightgown and put on her clothes. Then she gathered up her things at random, put them in the suitcase, and wrote a hurried note on a scrap of paper:

"Happiness was not made for people like me . . . Forgive me . . . My children are calling me . . . You wouldn't be happy living with half a woman . . . I know you . . ."

She looked at him one last time, with an expression that was both sad and determined. Then she went out and closed the door slowly, leaving behind dreams that were unattainable in the face of the reality that called her.

A Man and a Woman
RAFIQAT AL-TABIA

THE TWO OF THEM HAD BEEN STRETCHED OUT TOgether since the early hours of the evening. As the night wore on, the light of the bedside lamp grew bright around them. She was contrasting her dream with the miserable reality of the world:

"We are, then, *a man and a woman,* weaving love from old times. But neither your smiles, which I cherish, nor my whispers, which you desire, nor my kisses, nor your arms, nor our dreams together, can equal a single tear plucked by pain out of the round eyes set in this sad face, a face drained of all excitement.

"My eyes loved to embrace your picture every day, and memorize your features bit by bit. But one picture which I cut out recently, and the message written under it, have made me forget my joy with you. It was as if I had been brought back to the misery in which every human being is born, to the spontaneous cry that was in my mouth at birth, on the day when my only hope in life was the touch of the hands of the gentle midwife!

"Who are you from now on? Who am I? In my handbag I carry your personal papers—which contain love as *you* know it—and your picture. In your wonderful smile, which I adore, lies the image of the child with the round eyes. The child we used to dream of equally. *This* child, with the short message written under his picture, has eyes that cry without tears. Perhaps he's the child I used to wish you would give me one day, and now I've grown afraid of the mere thought of it. I'm a lost being. I don't own a foot of land here, or anywhere; and even if I do own a plot of land one day, what will it be worth when my turn comes, and I have to take your beautiful child in my arms and flee with him from the terror, only to throw him into perdition? Should I run with him to the south, to the blazing hot sands to bury him, his wide-open eyes, eager for life, sealed by the sandy storms? Or should I flee with him to the north, to drown him, the black lock of hair on his forehead plunged in the raging waves, his mouth filled with killer fish? Or do you want me to go east with him, to step on barbed wire that will sink into his soft, dark-skinned flesh, barking dogs and roaring weapons close behind us, as the flying dust covers us, suffocates us? I can see myself now, before the dark-skinned child is born, gathering up all the clothes I possess and dragging my feet around in search of a safe hut to shelter our child. A hut in which we would not be exposed to the howling winds that might blow away any fuel I had collected to warm my child's winter. I see myself struggling to find a tent of reeds to protect us from the midday summer sun, which might dissolve our child's nerves and dry out the blood of hope from my veins. I imagine the fog surrounding me in a strange, snowy territory, where I am utterly lost. I don't own a foot of land for my child, and your love isn't enough to fill with wealth and affection the vast world containing all the misery I now see in the eyes of the dark-skinned child, who cries without tears.

A Man and a Woman

"I no longer want a child. Hunger would kill him little by little. You would die away from him in a short, fateful battle. And I would spin around with him in a perpetual whirlpool of sadness. I don't want to give birth to a life and then kill it with my own hands. I don't want a child, born by me, to lead the life of a vagabond. I don't want to have to endure the pain suffered by an innocent creature who, because of me, was thrust into the agony of this world by the fates, a world that is threatened with hunger and nakedness and vagrancy. It is a world that smiles on millions of powerful people, while at the same time, and with the same calmness, sinking its poisonous claws into thousands of millions of faceless people. The child with the short message under his picture is dead. He was hungry, uprooted, sick. And with him my desire to give birth to a child has died forever.

"A dark-skinned child died, his feet burned by the blazing sands as he searched for a place of refuge like the one snatched from his parents. The death of a helpless child makes me sleepless, makes me abstain from you sometimes, shows me how insignificant are the hours that I regarded as immortal before.

"The picture of the homeless, hungry orphan crying without tears has made me put an end to my dreams before I start breathing life into them with you. Nothing will happen. We—you and I—will bury our dreams in their cradle with our own hands before the war buries them, or the earthquakes. Or before the tyranny of materialism kills them. After all, what are we but two repeated images!

"We are what is perhaps an inferior copy of the millions of copies which time has annihilated. *A man and a woman,* you and I. Behind us there are poor huts where the sick live, and in front of us tall buildings inhabited by hypocrisy. You and I are an insignificant link in the chain of time. It will not miss us. We used to dream of a future that never came and build on a past we couldn't remember. As for our present: the present is this picture of a lost child, without even a faint hope of finding a resting place, with no aspiration to feel even a false touch of affection from hands like mine or yours, with no expectation even of a mouthful of dry bread made from wheat which his parents had planted, but which dried out before ripening and bearing fruit.

"We are like the picture of the child I stumbled on, and the message under it. You plug your ears in order not to hear the misery in his voice. I shut my eyes, dreaming of the life of the gods, trying not to see the ugliness of life in our miserable present. Yet our child is the child in the picture. Why couldn't this child be ours? We bore him before today, before we were born ourselves. We bore him when we lived as a clearer copy in this world, before we died, and our souls returned to this miserable life in these two bodies we have grown accustomed to.

"Don't you remember you told me one day: 'When I was a child I used to feel older than my years?' Why couldn't it be that your *soul* was older? Your soul which was previously the soul of this father who died, unwillingly abandoning his poor son?

"Our child, then, has existed since olden times. We had the vain desire to repeat his birth through our dreams. What agony, my dear, have we suffered on account of his creation? What misery? Perhaps you will never love me again. My task had ended even before it began. My dream had died before it was born!

"It was as if my soul had grown old before all its youth was exhausted.

"I shall not give birth to a child, when there are poor children already everywhere, in the picture, and in reality, wandering in the desert, lost in woods, hungry in forests, ill in huts, orphaned and lonely on the shores of oceans and seas. I shall kill my dreams, my dear, and bury them before they take possession of us and lead us to increase the sadness of this world, to rob from it the mouthful of food belonging to a poor child who is already alive, in order to put it into the stomach of a child we used to dream of!"

Another Scarecrow
GHADA SAMMAN

IT'S RAINING. IT'S RAINING.
It's raining ash-gray hail, and boredom. It's been raining since morning, on and on, on and on.
I feel I'm in a slow train crossing vast, dead deserts. The passengers don't know each other; everyone speaks a different language; and no one knows where he's going, or where he's come from.
It's raining, dull, ceaseless rain.
In the garden, the cat wails continuously, a low, sorrowful wailing. It's like a sharp knife-blade sinking slowly and ceaselessly into my belly. I don't know why I dare not get rid of the cat, just as I don't know why I killed her kittens a few weeks ago.
During the night I had heard an appalling mewing. It was the first time I had heard my pampered cat wail like that. I followed the sound. I found her in my studio, near the window, and on the pillow were five little kittens, moving and squeaking. Five babies, just like that, and all at once! I don't know why I snatched them away, ignoring the claws clinging to my hands, or why I opened the window and threw all five of them out, one by one. The cat was still wailing, and in her eyes there was a dreadful accusing look. A human look, like that in the eyes of a woman whose children have been flayed in front of her.

An Arabian Mosaic

On the studio walls there were dozens of pictures of dozens of children. Their faces were alike, as if they were all the face of a particular child, a child who wasn't born yet, but whose features I knew very well. Even the men in my pictures had that child's face. Even the flowers. Even the things had the face of my still-to-be-born child. As I closed the door on the cat's wailing, I heard the hundreds of children in my pictures crying tears of bitterness and hatred.

It's raining. It's raining.

It's raining a new melancholy evening. If only the sky would explode with thunder and the clouds would burst open by lightning. If only the winds would roar and whistle in the cracks of the window. That would silence the cat and stop the terrible boredom. Anything, anything but the meaningless existence that dominates my days in this dreadful villa.

Despite the cold, he has been fixed, rigid and motionless, on the balcony for more than an hour, just as the scarecrow is fixed, rigid and motionless, at the bottom of the garden.

He's always silent. Since our marriage, we've exchanged words only rarely. I wonder if he speaks to the scarecrows and the ghosts of the garden. He takes out another cigarette. Why doesn't he offer the scarecrow a cigarette? In the first days of our marriage, this cold silence made me miserable. It threw me into a jaundiced, spiral maze in which even the echo would die. In the first days of our marriage, he was still capable of making me miserable. I would often search for an excuse for him, as I drew pictures of children, one after another, wishing that one day one of the pictures would scream and a

Another Scarecrow

living child would jump out of it. I could think of dozens of excuses: he's a judge, and in everything that goes on he judges me wrong. But he's also an important businessman. Perhaps that part of his personality has crept into our relationship. His feelings obey the law of supply and demand. If I frown, he smiles at me. If I am silent, he drowns me in unexpected eloquence. If I express desire for him, he rejects me; and if I turn away from him, his passion is aroused.

Then I learned how to burn the superfluous words of love on my lips, just as they burn coffee in Brazil so that its price will not go down.

I've become tired of the taste of ashes.

It's raining between my skin and my flesh. It's raining inside my bones, in my throat. I can't answer his question; it slaps against my face with the current of hail pouring in from the opened door.

"Did the doctor call with the result?"

"No . . . He didn't . . ."

"Who was it then? Who called?"

"It was them! They're waiting for you!"

I hear my voice, harsh and wounding.

"They're waiting for you!" I say it as if I were firing bullets at him. But he doesn't stagger, he doesn't drop dead. Instead he closes the balcony door behind him and goes out to his scarecrow. I hear myself repeating, "Them!" "Them!" "They're waiting for you!"

I see them there, waiting for him.

I see them there, ready. I see him come into the room, a combination of happy contradictions: the eyes of an old man and the smile of a child; the calm movement of a judge and the athletic appearance of a handsome businessman.

I see them scrutinize him. Then they will say many things. They will make grave accusations against him. They will talk voraciously, like crows tearing at the wounds of a man chained down and still alive.

He will not answer. I know he will not defend himself. He will confront them with the same coldness that has often burned me.

Then they will challenge him: they have a witness for the prosecution. He will laugh contemptuously. One of them will scream in his face: "We are sure of the accusation. You never studied a single defendant's file. You neglected everything—the legal proceedings, the prosecution, everything. You used to come to the courthouse with a bundle of folded papers in your pocket. On each paper you had written a single word: 'guilty' or 'innocent.' Your blind fingers would choose one paper from the darkness of your pocket. Then you would open it and read what was on it, 'guilty,' or 'innocent,' at random. Just like that, without logic or justification. This is no justice!"

And you will look at them attentively, smiling and silent.

Then the final blow will come: "The witness for the prosecution is your wife!" Perhaps only then will the gag fall from your mouth, and perhaps you will scream in their faces, just as you screamed in my face that fearful night a year ago.

It was also raining, but ferociously. I still loved you. I couldn't sleep if I couldn't hide my face in your chest. I

Another Scarecrow

still believed there were rare treasures at the bottom of the seas of your silence.

Light was shining from under the closed door of your office. I crept up on you, barefoot. I had decided to persuade you to come to bed by planting a kiss on the back of your neck. I moved up behind you slowly and silently. Then I stopped. As I was about to bend over and kiss you, I caught sight of something that stunned me. On the desk were dozens of scraps of paper with nothing written on them except the word "guilty" or "innocent." And the black book you had brought with you and said you were going to study was lying on the floor, under your feet!

I groaned. When you turned to me, and I saw the dreadful expression on your face, I understood everything. In an instant, like a flash of lightning, I understood everything. Your face remained contracted, dripping sweat. So that was what your silence was hiding! Despite your great success in business, you had hung on to your position as a judge in order to kill, and to do so from behind a veil! Your face advanced toward me. I remembered the faces described in Dante's Hell. I was afraid. I wanted to run away. You held my hands tightly, pinning me down. I tried to escape but couldn't. I felt I had somehow been sentenced to death. But you would never dare carry out the sentence yourself.

"You wouldn't dare!"

"You, fool!"

"You wouldn't dare . . . This time it would be a crime that leaves blood and a corpse behind . . ."

"You, fool!"

"And you couldn't do it in the name of justice . . ."

"You, fool!"
"And you won't get paid for committing it!"
"You, fool! That's terrible . . . terrible . . ."
"You're supposed to represent the justice of the gods."
"I apply it in their way . . . Try to understand."
"That's heresy. What can the gods be to blame for in this?"
"I honestly try to do as they would do."
"And leave people's fate to random chance?"
"Chance rules the world."
"You're crazy!"
"And you're a fool. You're still deceived by the game."

Then I convinced myself that I was no longer deceived by the game, that I had to do something to save my ideals and the thousands of accused people whose fate was being decided by chance. But when he ordered that something should be done to scare the birds in the garden, I came to the painful conclusion that perhaps I was doing all this because my husband didn't speak to me, because the dead silence had made my life an empty desert. Even mourning a dead person is better than waiting for a joy that will never come!

The telephone rings. Perhaps it's the doctor. Perhaps he has good news for me. I stay stock-still. I don't want to move. I'm afraid it might be "them," those who are "waiting for him." The maid, Tuffaha, rolls along the hall, carrying her swollen belly in front of her. She lifts the receiver. She mumbles. She comes toward me, holding the receiver in one hand. How ugly she is! Ugly! With her dead, expressionless face, her step like that of a farm

Another Scarecrow

bull, and that belly. I watch that belly swelling, growing bigger day by day. Why aren't its muscles ripped apart? Why doesn't it drop to the ground and smash to pieces? How could any man in the world make love to such a beast? How disgusting to think of them. I hate her. It tears me apart to imagine there's a little child inside the shabby clothes that envelop her huge form. And it belongs to her! Whereas I, with all that I possess, and with all the men who eye me hungrily—I cannot have anything like this!

A few minutes pass, and I let the receiver fall from my hand.

So, I will never have a child! Never, never, never . . .

The doctor has now told me. The decision is final, not open to partiality or reversal.

Why? He doesn't know. Nobody knows.

Why?

Above a cloud stretching to a dark horizon, I see the hundreds of papers I saw before on my husband's desk: "guilty," "innocent," "barren," "fertile," "guilty," "innocent," "barren," "fertile" . . . Then devilish, jesting fingers pick up one paper. Then the doctor says: "Sorry, you're barren." And on the pillow the cat had borne them all at once, five babies.

Barren. Perhaps the scarecrow had children like itself, but they hated the silence, and so flew off with the songs of the birds of the fields.

It's raining. It's raining.

It's raining a low moaning that rises slowly, so slowly, merging with the wailing of the cat in the garden . . . We are three scarecrows, each of us fixed far away from the other, never conversing, never meeting. Who is it that's moaning?

He comes in from the balcony. He doesn't seem to hear any unusual voice. He says he's going out but won't be back late.

As usual, he doesn't hear any moaning. He goes off, and I see torn papers flying under his feet, "guilty," "innocent," "guilty," "innocent" . . .

I'm alone in the house.

The moaning rises. Who is it that's moaning? It's all in my imagination. There's no one in the isolated villa except me, and the maid. Tonight Beirut hasn't turned its lights on, one after the other, in the corners of the windows. The fog, like a whale, has swallowed it up. Perhaps the scarecrow is weeping. I wonder if it gets sad or angry. Does it ever feel hatred or revolt? Does it talk to my husband, Najm? Does it sneak into the office every night on its cane legs and sit with him? Do the two of them tear up the papers together and write "guilty," "innocent" . . . ? Why don't silent men marry scarecrows? Why am I condemned unjustly to silence? Why is there no child to fill the place, screaming in protest, tearing off the veil from Najm's face?

It's raining. It's raining.

The moaning turns into punctuated screams. Perhaps the children in my pictures are hungry. Until now, I haven't found a way to feed them. Perhaps they need to go for a walk, and play. My children are prisoners in the pictures. Why don't the gods free them, let them burst into the world from my insides, from my belly?

It's raining screams . . .

Another Scarecrow

Who's screaming like that? Perhaps the body in the picture whose face I haven't yet drawn is protesting.

I run to my studio. I turn on the light. There's nothing. There's no one except my twenty children, nailed to the walls, and the picture, still incomplete, awaiting a face. The window is open. The pillow on which the cat gave birth to her kittens lies in its place. I dare not approach the window. I have the impression that behind it, outside in the darkness, there are five little cats lurking, their fangs pointed. If I look out, they will sink their claws into my face and tear it apart.

I run away.

It's still raining screams. I know where the voice is coming from. It's calling my name. It's not my imagination. I hate Sunday night, when all the servants have gone away. Tuffaha is the only one who hasn't been given time off since I noticed her belly growing. I hate her, and I hate the patient way she endures my torture. I want her to stay *here*. I don't know why I like to oppress her. I see her gasping with fatigue, wiping away her smelly sweat, moving like a stupid animal, and I try in vain to convince myself that there's a goat in her belly, or a cub, or mice . . .

I look in the kitchen. She isn't there.

I make my way to her miserable room. She's stretched out on her back on the bed. Her hands are on her big belly. She's silent. The muscles of her face are still contracted with a pain I've never seen before on her features. Her face is pathetic and horrifying!

At her side are the hooks I've often seen her working with, weaving garment after garment. I've seen the delicate hands of little children come out of the openings of the unfinished garments as they grow day by day with the continuous needlework. I feel an infuriating urge to sink the hooks into her belly. I will sink them in until they tear her insides apart and destroy her womb. Why is she screaming? The hooks are still in their place. She opens her eyes for a second, and a terrible look of feminine triumph flashes across them. Her eyes challenge me. Then they drown in a dark sea of pain mingled with strange pleasure that draws over her face—the pain of a nun who is being raped and is tormented by the sense of pleasure that it gives her.

She mumbles, pleadingly. She wants a doctor.

Why? Why should the doctor come for her sake and not for mine? And for the child that is hers and not mine?

Something black wells up from the depths of me and merges with her crying. Black bubbles form. They rise up, gush out from my throat, my eyes, my pores. Black bubbles of burning acid submerge everything. Everything is torn, burning. I want everything to be torn, to burn. I want to protest, to revolt, to engulf everything around me in senseless destruction. Why? Why? Who? Who? How? When? Who? Who passed this sentence on me? Why shall I never stretch out on the bed and get up with a child in my arms? Why shall I not feel the kicking of little feet in my belly, and the body of a child turning over inside me, then wake up from my sleep to touch him until his screaming fills up the house?

I gaze at her with a dead face, hoping the black bubbles will gush out from my eyes and drown her. Why? Who? Who? Who plays with the papers, scattering them in the wind, to be carried away by blind chance, marked "barren" or "fertile"? Is Najm to blame for being so quick

Another Scarecrow

to grasp the fact? Is he to blame for believing in his heresy and being devoted to his calamity?

It's raining. The rain falls outside the window. I wonder if it's also raining in Beirut. Why doesn't it rain everywhere at the same time?

Who decides where the rain falls and where the children come? Who has made chance into justice?

It's raining. It's raining.

The maid screams, pleading. For weeks she's been begging for time off. She must have known.

I stay stock-still, exploding with black hatred. I'll bury her with black bubbles. I'll pile earth on her like a grave, and choke the screams of the child inside her. Her pain provokes something like jealousy in me, but much more bitter, more stinging, more miserable.

She becomes quiet, half-unconscious. I have the urge to draw a child! Let her give birth to her child by herself. I have nothing to do with it. I shall go to my studio and give birth to a new child as well. I shall finish that picture. I shall ignore what the doctor said on the phone. Her screaming starts up again, then turns to crying.

Let her scream. No one will ever hear her in our secluded house in al-Yarze.[1] Let her die. If she manages to give birth like the cat did, I won't dare throw the child out of the window. I won't dare because since tonight I no longer see the looks of love and friendship with which the faces of the children in my pictures used to envelop me. They've begun to frown at me; they've stopped their nighttime singing. They've started to hate me, and fear

---

[1] An exclusive neighborhood in Beirut, with villas surrounded by spacious gardens.

me. I will bear a new child now. I will lay it down on the paper and get rid of all the others.

The maid's moaning stirs a similar wailing in the depths of me, a wailing of black bubbles, a raging current of tense, impetuous, acid screams. I feel the urge to draw. My hand races ahead of me, pulling me to the studio. I'm a prisoner of my hand. The black current moves my hand. The maid's screaming provokes it. I'm incapable of controlling a single muscle in my body. My hand is drawing on its own, madly, frantically. Outside, it's raining ferociously. The maid's screams are like the cries of a sailor cast up on the shore, being eaten by crabs. My hand is drawing on its own, madly, frantically . . .

It's raining ferociously. The thunder sounds like a minefield high above, being set off by devilish feet. Lightning flashes. I'm afraid. The maid screams. I'm afraid. Afraid. I feel something on the back of my neck. The claws of vicious cats. I feel them tearing at my flesh. I'm afraid. Out in the field, millions of scarecrows are marching. They're carrying torches in a terrifying ceremonial procession. The thunder sounds like one vast minefield. The lightning flashes periodically, setting alight the children on the walls. I draw. I want to draw a child, but I don't know what I'm drawing. The scarecrows advance toward the window. The electricity fails. The children in my pictures suddenly grow huge. The lightning strikes the faces with their gouged-out eyes. The faces freeze, their teeth fall to the floor, their hair turns white, they weep. Then they change into more scarecrows. They jump down from the pictures and out of the open window, joining the throng singing under it.

Another Scarecrow

Their weeping-singing screams have a terrible rhythm. Meanwhile, the wind beats against the window. I want to run away. I can't. My hand chains me to the picture. So I draw on and on, and I can't run away. The electricity is back. I can't run away. Then suddenly one scream rings out at the door of my studio.

It's the other woman, leaving a trail of blood behind her.

The screaming of the procession outside quiets down. It seems as if millions of scarecrows are now peering furtively through the windows, staring with their gouged-out eyes, silent, timidly submissive. The other woman braces herself, comes in, and drops onto the chair, and onto the very same pillow on which the cat gave birth to five babies. I wonder if she too will give birth to five babies.

She seems huge, so huge to me. A great giant. In her eyes there is a commander's challenge, an amazing creative power, inexplicable, and a pain that is beautiful and radiating and bitter.

I begin to be conscious of things again.

A cruel, calamitous calmness fills me.

She wants a doctor or else she will die.

I'm the absolute ruler.

I try in vain to remember my ideals. I try in vain to re-awaken in myself my sweet old world. I search in vain for the face I once had.

In the picture that I've drawn unconsciously, I find a strange face, a mixture of my face and Najm's face! A mixture of cruelty and calamity, even of indifference. The picture suddenly seems like a mirror to me. I smile, and the face in the picture smiles. I move my lips, and the face moves its lips.

The moaning turns to screaming and rises up to me again. What sentence shall I pass? The frost of calamitous cruelty fills me. It becomes petrified inside me. At the threshold of my world all the voices die in utter silence. I go out to my husband's office. I sit down where he sat. I take out a blank sheet of paper. I cut it carefully into two equal parts. On one piece I write "I shall bring the doctor" and on the other "I shall not bring the doctor." I fold each of them, I put them in my pocket, I muddle them up.

Then I take one of them out.

I open it and read: "I shall not bring the doctor." The decision is final, irrevocable. I can't hear any voices when I go into my room. I dress calmly and carefully. I pick up my car keys. I take care to leave my husband a note: "I'm with Nura and Nilly. We're going to play bridge with the rest of the group."

The Second and the Truth
Khayriyya al-Saqqaf

THOSE WERE SPRING DAYS . . .
Just like the spring days which had gone before . . . She wasn't very interested in measuring the time—the months, weeks, or days, the hours, minutes, or seconds . . .

She stood for a few moments, caught in the scheme of time, near a wall on which a huge clock was hanging.

It was a clock like those magnificent ones made in previous generations—old, wooden, with an air of authenticity and gravity, and matching the shadowy awesomeness of the house.

She looked at him. She thought for a long time why it was she had never tried to speak to him.

He was fifty years old. He sat on a swivel chair, wearing a wide gown. His head was covered with a piece of cloth whose original color she couldn't discern, because it was faded with age; it was neither round nor oblong, of a hue tending toward black. His eyes looked out from behind a pair of thick glasses. He was holding a book between his hands.

I go away and come back at night or in the daytime. A week passes, or a month, and I always find him in the same position, with the same book between his hands, open at the same page. I remember growing up seeing

An Arabian Mosaic

him just like that, just as if he were one of the ornaments in the house; but whereas some of the ornaments have been changed or rearranged, and some have been lost, he remains just as he was! And behind him the big round clock still hangs on the wall. It too has stopped at one particular point: it always says 5 minutes and 25 seconds to 5!!!

She had come on one of those spring days. She sat down slowly beside him, and began to speak to him.

He didn't answer. He remained silent, speechless.

"How is it spring goes away and summer comes, and then autumn begins, and one year goes by and is followed by another, and you sit in the same place, in the same clothes and shoes, with the same glasses on, holding the same book?!"

He didn't answer . . . He remained silent.

"Has time stood still at 5 minutes and 25 seconds to 5? Or do you perhaps think of the world as nothing but a book between your hands, a book called *Life Is a Second*?"

She asked her questions without expecting any reply, then she got up to leave.

But for the first time ever, he cleared his throat and moved in his chair. It came as a shock to her, because he had never done this before. Then he tested his voice with one low cough and then another, as though he were trying it out for the first time after a long period of imprisonment and enduring silence.

He said:

"It seems to me you haven't grasped the meaning of the passage of time. That's why I didn't answer your

The Second and the Truth

question before. *(You stupid girl. You'll understand as time goes on . . .)*

"I didn't bother to answer your second question because it isn't worth the trouble. *(You stupid girl. Perhaps you don't understand the eloquence of silence!)*

"As for your third question, the first part is beyond you, because you don't understand the true nature of the hour and its minutes and seconds; and the last part came to an end the very second I spoke."

And he fell silent. He froze. His pulse stopped.

She shook him, screamed, beat his face with the palms of her hands.

She stared at him, stunned. He didn't move.

She stepped back, terrified. *Could he have been a real man after all, a normal human being? What was it he wanted to say and I didn't understand?!*

Perhaps man reaches a stage of contentment with his personal philosophy, then dissolves and dies. And when he stops at the stage of profound comprehension of this philosophy, perhaps he cannot realize his own value unless he is able to draw attention to himself and bring someone else to a stop . . . At that point, does he perhaps not care if he comes to an end and wastes away, or if he remains and goes on?

She looked at the clock.

She was utterly afraid . . . distraught. She saw that the clock had moved on one more second: it was now 5 minutes and 26 seconds to 5 . . .

She backed away, petrified, slapping her hands against the wall.

Fragments from a Life

SHARIFA AL-SHAMLAN

First Fragment

I'm twenty years old, I'm sure. My mother died when I was ten. I was brought here when I was seventeen. I used to calculate my age by planting a date tree every year. I've been here three years—which I know from my father's visits. At the end of every Ramadan he visits me three times.

Another Fragment

Today's the eve of a religious festival. Tomorrow's the festival. Our place is being decorated not because of the festival, but because the director will visit us.

I requested a pen and some paper. I wanted to write a long letter to my mother and a card wishing my father a happy festival. They refused my request. They were afraid I would write a complaint and give it to the director. I laughed at them a lot in my heart, because I don't know how to write at all . . .

And Another Fragment

I laughed a lot when I looked at the director. He seemed puffed up, puffed up very, very much. The male nurses lined up on either side of him, clean and neat. When the director approached me, the chief doctor whispered audibly in his ear: "She's dangerous."

I tried to stretch out my hand to feel the director's gown. A smile spread across his lips and he said: "What do you want, young girl?"

"To touch your gown," I said.

"Why?"

I told him to get closer, then I whispered in his ear: "I want to see how much it would be worth if it were sold. Would it be enough to buy candy for the children in my village?"

He laughed, and went away.

The chief doctor was frightened. His eyes were popping.

A Back Fragment

The sight of the chief doctor makes me laugh. He has maps on his face that I drew with my fingernails. One day he wanted to break my pride. I tried to break his nose, but I didn't succeed. All I did was paint his face with his blood.

A Small Fragment

The maid handed me my food. I didn't ask her anything about herself. She said: "I gave the meat to the neighbors' dog. It was hungry."

"Did the dog deserve it?" I asked.

Fragments from a Life

A Cross-Sectioned Fragment

The nurse comes as usual. In her hand there is an injection. Instead of inserting it in my arm, she empties it into another vial, which she promptly hides in the front of her dress. I don't care. True, the injection takes me to beautiful worlds, to a vast universe, but afterward it leaves me in a dark world—and with a terrible headache.

I told the nurse that I would like her to bring me a lot of palm branches.

"Why?" she asked with indifference.

"I will make a fence from them around my bed," I said.

She gasped. She folded her apron carefully, and went off in a rush.

A Painful Fragment

One day my father bought me bracelets. I was very happy with them. I showed them off to my friends. My father's wife bought necklaces, and anklets, and many bracelets. I didn't mind. I was happy because my father had become rich. I sat down looking at my bracelets. They glittered. They glittered when they reflected the rays of the sun. I heard a loud noise . . . A big—huge—bulldozer was digging up the garden . . . It was approaching my date trees . . . I screamed. . . . I screamed . . . I ran . . . I sat down on the ground in front of it . . . My father's wife dragged me away. She said: "We've sold the garden. They're going to turn it into a road."

I pulled her hair. I scratched her face. She said: "Don't you want to know where the bracelets came from?"

An Arabian Mosaic

I threw the bracelets under the big bulldozer. After that, I was brought here . . .

Last Fragment

The maid said to me: "They wrote about you in the newspapers."

"Why?" I asked.

"The director had sent candy to the children in your village."

"Were the children happy?"

"Yes," she said. "They sent a telegram of thanks to the director."

Pharaoh Is Drowning Again

SAKINA FUAD

THE SEA. I TRAVEL ABOVE YOU TO THE END OF THE world. I came from you as a drop, as a tear from your eye. Why was crying created from tears? So that I would fall as a tear? A tear on a night of love, or a night of misery, or a night of revenge. Any night. A man and a woman and a tear. And a creature dying and living, carrying the sin of one night. Life in its entirety is the sin of one night. Damned are the nights which produce human beings. They drink in the nights infused with anxiety. Misery flows in the marrow of their bones. The shock occurs every moment. The electric touch of pain is embedded in the folds of the brain. Creatures afflicted by madness, anger, agony, and frustration, and ground down by the crush, the chase, and the fleeing.

From where? And to where? And when will the drop return to the sea? I don't know.

The voice of the singer Abd al-Wahab cries in the distance, carrying all the sorrows of the night.

The sea . . .

Moses struck the water with his stick. The water receded, and a way was opened up beneath the feet of those fleeing.

An Arabian Mosaic

I was one of them. I hid myself in the exodus of the wretched and covered myself with their nights in order to flee. I was lost in their perdition. We descended into the bottom of the parted sea, crawled, and fled. The waves protected us. The waves were like mountains on either side of us. It was a moment in which the whole world became still. The sea held its breath. Had it breathed, the mountains of its waves would have tumbled down on those in flight. The sea held its breath and clutched its waves to its heart. We crossed to the other bank. We flung ourselves onto the ground to catch our breath, to nurse the wounds, and to still the pain with the sweetness of salvation.

The sense of terror . . .

The sight of Pharaoh standing on the other bank with his armies of men and chariots, his arrows sharpened and poisoned . . .

The flight . . .

But where to? There is no escape. Pharaoh is our fate. He is always behind us.

Then who is the way for?

"Whoever wants to escape will find a way."

There's no end to my good mother's proverbs. Life consists of pleasing proverbs on my mother's tongue, and other women's tongues.

My mother is a person from the generation of proverbs. Her words, which have no meaning, are killing me. When they reach my ears, I feel as if they chop off my head and blow out my brains. I raise a hue and cry in her face, and in my face, and in the face of the whole world.

I run away . . .

"Taxi!"

Pharaoh Is Drowning Again

"Where to? . . . What's the address?"

"Take me as close as you can to the sea."

The taxi takes off at full speed. My mind races ahead of the speeding car to the water. My innermost feelings are a sea raging and beating against the shores of my body. I head off from wherever I may be sitting, and sail away. The horizon has no limits. The world has no end. I came to the world at the moment of beginning. Everything was water, and I was a drop, swirling with the current, gliding on the surface of the universe. The earth and the sky were still joined together. I was at their meeting point. I disengaged myself. I climbed up to the sky and down to the earth. I chose the sea, so that the journey and the horizon would remain my limitless world. I could climb to the sky and flow on the surface of the earth. There were no limits and no fetters, no bridges and no walls. We were all drops, swimming and swimming. When did the journey of misery begin?

The drop was covered with white foam. The foam became a beautiful woman. Her first name was Aphrodite. The name changed and the form changed too, but she remained a woman. The body is only the first prison cell. After this prison, there are millions of others.

"Whereabouts?" The driver asks again.

And I'm still traveling alone, competing with the speeding car, searching for a time where cares and sorrows have vanished; looking for a place that doesn't possess me, nor I it; a place that I come to as a guest and leave without grief, without being known, and without knowing it.

The silence takes me back from the sea to the earth. The silence means we've come to a stop.

An Arabian Mosaic

"Whereabouts?"

"This is the place."

I look closely at the number, at the building, at the faces. Everything is as it used to be. I stare at the driver. How did he know my address and bring me to my door?

I ask him.

He assures me I gave him the address when I flung myself on the car seat. I don't argue.

A lot of things have come to an end, including the age of arguing. We've entered the age of silence. Everything is done by force of habit. All actions take place without the intervention of our will. We eat. We drink. We sleep. Children are born. We kill, and hate, and love. Even love. What was the meaning of this word in your time, you, the old people? Words are few. We can no longer bear the additional burden of the word. Machines operate and think and plan. The radio is the only machine that sometimes speaks. There are modern devices that pick up vibrations from space. Our engineers work away, and receivers break through new barriers every day. Voices are received from space, and we hear all those who have left us. I have no longing for anyone. I've often asked about the meaning of this word. They say longing is a cold that bites at the depths of the heart. Longing is a mad craving for something. These words belong to the age of words: my heart is nothing but a pump drawing blood.

This morning is different from any other morning . . . Why?

In a vibrating, staccato voice, the radio broadcaster announces:

"Our instruments have managed to pick up signals—

Pharaoh Is Drowning Again

muttering and whispering—from the uppermost reaches of space. Reception is still poor, but the voices have confirmed that they are from our planet, from earth. Everything is still very vague. We are trying to overcome engineering problems, but the few words that have reached us are ones of greeting to you."

For the first time ever, longing is born in me. My blood's pump trembles; the monotonous routine to which it has worked, year in, year out, breaks down.

The cold that bites at the depths of the heart . . .

I yearn for something . . .

My yearnings are submerged in a feeling of alienation. I don't know what he wants, or what I want. I listen to the program. Instruments have been used that are more sensitive than any known before. No penetration of space has ever reached these voices before. This is the first time *they* have said that *they* leave us simply to dissolve in space as souls, and then observe us. I throw myself to the floor at the foot of this sophisticated piece of equipment. My ears vie with the instruments in trying to reach out into space. I search for something.

These mutterings and buzzings and silences and tears are all his. I heard his tears and silence and coughing as he met the morning with his old, bare chest. He died far away from us. They said it happened in obscure circumstances. His pointed words killed him. In an age when only sickly words are spoken, he was surrounded by sugar-coated words. But he was not one of those who spoke them.

I've never seen him. I know him as if he breathes in my soul, and I wear his face, with all its sharp features.

My mother tells me I was born a few days after they

took him away. But I know him. His image appears to me often. I meet him on all my journeys. There is no shore I visit without seeing him there as well. His roaring laughter is soundless. He beats his broad chest and waves his fist. One day the time for our meeting will come. And today I hear him. My heart is heavy with longing. Its fuse can explode at a touch. The sand from every shore of every sea in the whole wide world will no longer be enough to extinguish the fire.

"Where to?"

To whom is my question addressed? I can't find the taxi driver. When did I get out of the taxi? How long does it take to climb these twenty floors with their five hundred stairs? I don't count them with time or numbers, but with the words that are gnawing at my heart and that I'm chewing over. I finally reach the last floor. People, houses, cars are like little toys fulfilling the daily routine. At the end of the day the puppets are turned over, their faces down. The game at night is called sleep. At dawn, the key is stealthily turned, and the machines are wound up and begin to gyrate. I've released my daily scream. Who will release me from my key? Who will break the prison cells? Who will make me a human being again?

My heart pumps longing. The face of my father, whom I've never seen, accompanies me. I wait for his voice in the coming vibrations. I thirst for it. I touch all the seas of the world and they turn into crystals.

I want a drop of water.

My apartment is on the first floor. I won't go back there. I've taken the decision for the thousandth time. I climb up and down the five hundred stairs every day, struggling with the decision and fleeing from my chained

Pharaoh Is Drowning Again

will. The turning of the key in the elegant door puts an end to everything. There it is: the air-conditioned apartment, the colorful walls, the soft white bed on which dreams roam and stretch and yawn. The plushness and lushness of the bedroom are enticing. My husband conducts his important conversations on a number of colorful phones. Everything is soft, alluring, and entwined in fine spiderwebs. The expensive pictures are imported from Paris. He draws his money from an enchanted well. His hobby is to collect the rare—in art, in love, in food.

He laughs ironically. What is left of my breath, after the exertion of climbing the stairs, fails at the sight of the triumphant expression on his face. My dead resolution finds its resting place in his eyes. I've become part of the picture. The comfort and softness possess me. The silence, the stillness, the smoothness drag me to the bottom of the earth. I sink under its layers. The spiderwebs wrap my feet together, twisting my steps round themselves. I turn round and spin between the rooms. The tombstones of furniture rise higher every day. I recite the verses of the Fatiha.[1] The reciting voice rings out in the silence. The walls close in. They move, advance, press together. They turn my body into a flat, dry surface, a leaf preserved for millions of years between the pages of a book made of brick, concrete, and iron. My heart pumps longing. I rewind the recorded program. I listen. My ears reach out into space searching for him, for his roar, for the blow he struck into the air in order to crush them, for the spit he spat at them when they

---

[1] The first chapter of the Koran, which is recited, among other occasions, at funerals or when remembering the dead or on visiting a grave.

An Arabian Mosaic

took him away. He spoke his words at the right time. Words that are not spoken at the right place and time are decaying bodies.

My body leaves the bed, emptying what is inside it. My husband makes love to me skillfully, as skillfully as he handles everything else I don't know about. The cup of tea, the rocking chair which is moving monotonously, the long bathrobe and the bed are all still warm. I tremble and watch his briefcase. The briefcase walks away, carried by his hand. It disappears. I, and the other things in the picture, go into a state of waiting.

I tidy everything up again, but without deviating one step from the framework of the picture. The tombstones of furniture rise higher every day. I move round them, reciting the verses of the Fatiha. I lift the silk covers. There is not a scratch on the furniture. The covers are lifted only to be patted gently and to have the dust brushed off them. His hobby is to visit auctions and bring back the rarest things. He visited our house and handed his money over, and I was added to his purchases and the collection of rare things. My features have become the same as theirs. Words have lost their value. Silence is no longer a condition around us: silence is a living creature inhabiting our depths and smothering every ember there. Everything is done by force of habit or through fear of him. Pharaoh runs his kingdom with great skill; the maids are sent to the market and the wives are kept behind closed doors. Pharaoh is a lord who rules by divine right. The queen ascends a throne of fog; a puff of air from the master's mouth blows the throne away and he seats another woman on his right or on his left. Kingship has corrupted everything. Sincerity has

Pharaoh Is Drowning Again

died out and the warmth of things has faded away. Pharaoh does not speak. Pharaoh has become one of the machines of our time, operating, pushing buttons, managing.

This morning is different from any other morning . . . Why? Penetration into outer space brings back all those who have left us. Penetration into the layer where souls live is happening for the first time. I've recorded the program. I play the recording again at the lowest speed, searching for him among them. Everything strong belongs to him, the laughter, the roaring, the stupefying silence.

He says his words here. I long for him. I long for the word. I long for a place that doesn't possess me nor I it. I move. I dart along, without limitations, without chains. I dwell on the surface of the whole world, taking and giving. I turn into a drop of water. I flow into the big sea.

The sea . . .

Pharaoh is standing on the other bank. His scream reverberates. I must go home, or else he will come down to fetch me.

Pharaoh goes down to the bottom of the parted sea.

The wounds dry out. The pains subside. I stand upright on the shore of the wretched. I turn into a giant rebel, killing and burning. The waves roar. The sea releases the breath it has been holding till we cross. Its mountains explode as raging waves, submerging Pharaoh and his armies. They beat the water with their hands; their chests fill up with brine; their remains float on the water.

The world quiets down. It becomes empty, clear.

We are at the moment of beginning.

I'm still moving as I sit on the ground, watching the

An Arabian Mosaic

sea: the movement of the water takes me on a journey across the whole world. My heart is a bird that has left my breast to flutter on a horizon where the earth joins the sky. My body is a ship that stops at harbors to take provisions, then continues its travels.
I will not return . . . until the sea has swallowed all the Pharaohs.

Biographical Notes on Authors

Ulfa al-Idilbi A Syrian author, born in 1912 in Damascus. She has published four collections of short stories and a novel, *Damascus: A Smile of Sorrow*, which was made into a movie by the Syrian Cinema Institute. The story "The Breeze of Youth" ("Nasamat al-Siba") is from the collection *Wada'an Ya Dimashq* (Damascus, 1963).

Ihsan Kamal An Egyptian fiction writer, born in 1935. She has many collections of short stories to her credit, and has twice won the Story Contest of the Story Club in Egypt: in 1957, and in 1960. Several of her stories have been made into film and television productions. The story "A Mistake in the Knitting" ("Satr Maghlut") is the title story of a collection published in Cairo in 1971.

Alifa Rifaat An Egyptian author, born in 1930 in Cairo. She was brought up as a devout Muslim, and because of her early marriage did not pursue formal education after secondary school. She has traveled widely in Egypt with her husband, a police officer. First published under a pseudonym, her work has, since 1972, been published under her own name. Several of her stories have been translated into English. The story "My Wedding Night" ("Hadhihi Laylati") is from the collection *Man Yakun al-Rajul?* (Cairo, 1981).

Biographical Notes

Samira Azzam (1927–1967) A Palestinian short-story writer who, from 1948 until her death, lived in Lebanon and Iraq. She published four collections of short stories; the fifth appeared posthumously. Her volume *The Hour and the Man* (1963) won the prize of the Lebanese Association of Friends of the Book. The story "Tears for Sale" ("Dumu' lil-Bay' ") is from the collection *al-Zil al-Kabir* (Beirut, 1956).

Daisy al-Amir An Iraqi short-story writer, born in 1935 in Basra. She has a bachelor's degree from the Teachers' Training College in Baghdad. In 1963 she went to Beirut and chose to stay there, first working as an employee of the Iraqi embassy, then as Director of the Iraqi Cultural Center. She has published several collections of short stories in which, as in the one translated here, she voices her response to the civil war. The story "The Future" ("al-Mustaqbal") is from the collection *Fi Dawwamat al-Hubb wa al-Karahiya* (Beirut, 1979). The story "The Cat, the Maid, and the Wife" ("al-Qitta wa al-Khadima wa al-Zawja") is from the collection *Wu'ud lil-Bay'* (Beirut, 1981).

Hanan al-Shaykh A Lebanese fiction writer from a conservative Shiite-Muslim family, born in 1947. She received her secondary education in Beirut, and in 1963 went to the American College for Girls in Cairo, where she stayed for four years and wrote her first novel. She traveled to Saudi Arabia, then went back to Lebanon, but after the outbreak of the civil war she left for England and settled in London. She has published three novels and a volume of short stories. The story "The Persian Rug" ("al-Sajjada al-'Ajamiyya") is from the collection *Wardat al-Sakhra'* (Beirut, 1982).

Biographical Notes

Nawal al-Saadawi A leading feminist writer, born in Egypt in 1930. She received a degree in medicine from Cairo University, then served as a physician in various public posts, including Director of Health Education in the Ministry of Health. She has published several novels, collections of short stories, and social studies, of which *Woman and Sex* and *The Hidden Face of Eve* have gained much publicity. Under Sadat's regime, she was imprisoned for several months on account of her political views and activities. Her books have been translated into a number of European languages. The story "The Picture" ("al-Sura") is from the collection *Kanat Hiya al-Ad'af* (Beirut, 1979).

Latifa al-Zayat An Egyptian writer, born in 1945. She holds a master's degree in English literature from Cairo University, and a doctorate in translation from the University of Ein Shams, where she works as a professor. She has published critical studies on English literature, and on the Egyptian novel and Egyptian drama. Her fiction includes a novel entitled *al-Bab al-Maftuh* (1960), and a volume of short stories entitled *al-Shuykhukha wa Qisas Ukhra* (Cairo, 1986). The story "The Picture" ("al-Sura") is from that volume.

Layla al-Uthman A Kuwaiti fiction writer, born in 1945. Her formal education did not extend beyond secondary school, but she expanded it by wide reading in Arabic and in Western literature. Considered a leading woman writer in the Arabian Peninsula, she has published two novels and several collections of short stories. The story "The Picture" ("al-Sura") is from the collection *Fi al-Layl Ta'ti al-'Uyun* (Beirut, 1980).

May Ziyada (1895–1941) A Palestinian writer, born

Biographical Notes

and educated in Nazareth. Her father, a well-known Lebanese journalist, took his family to Egypt in 1908 and settled in Cairo. She is considered a pioneer woman writer in modern Arabic literature. Her literary output is varied and includes essays, poems, and short stories. The story "The Lady with the Story" ("Hikayat al-Sayyida Allati Laha Hikaya") is from a posthumous publication entitled *Sawanih Fata* (Beirut, 1975). This is the first story by her to appear in English.

Layla Bin Mami A Tunisian fiction writer, born in Djebra in 1944. She studied in Tunis and received three degrees in Arabic. She writes in Arabic. The appearance of her collection of short stories, provocatively entitled *A Burning Minaret* (*Sawma'a Tahtariq*; Tunis, 1968), created an uproar similar to that caused by Layla Baalbakki's *A Spaceship of Tenderness to the Moon*. The story "I Want Him a Free Man" ("Uriduhu Hurran") is from the above-mentioned collection. This is her first appearance in English.

Kulit Suhayl al-Khuri A Syrian poet, novelist, and short-story writer, born in 1937 in Damascus. She comes from a wealthy Catholic family and was educated both in Arabic and in French. Her poetry is written in French, but the fiction—short stories and novels—in Arabic. She currently lectures at the University of Damascus. The story "Where To?" ("Ila Ayna?") is from the collection *Ana wa al-Mada* (Beirut, 1962).

Layla Baalbakki A Lebanese fiction writer from a conservative Shiite-Muslim family, born in 1936. Her first novel, *I Live*, has been translated into French and other European languages. She has published another novel, and a collection of short stories entitled *A Space-*

Biographical Notes

ship of Tenderness to the Moon (*Safinat Hanan ila al-Qamar*; Beirut, 1963). The stories landed her in court on charges of obscenity and damaging public morality, but she was eventually acquitted. The story "The Cat" ("al-Qitta") is from the above-mentioned collection.

Hayat Ibn al-Shaykh A Tunisian author, born in 1943 in Tunis. She writes in Arabic and has published poetry and fiction. Her first collection of short stories, *Without a Man* (*Bi-la Rajul*), appeared in Tunis in 1979. It was followed by another collection, *Tomorrow the Sun of Freedom Will Rise* (*Wa Ghadan Tushriq Shams al-Hurriyya*) in 1983. The story "A Woman Worth Less than Nothing" ("Imra'a taht al-Sifr") is from the first collection. This is her first appearance in English.

Sufi Abdallah An Egyptian writer from a conservative Muslim background, born in 1925 in al-Fayyum. She studied in French, English, and Italian schools, and began to publish in 1942 by contributing essays and short stories to different journals and magazines. In 1955 she became the editor of the column "Your Problem" in the women's magazine *Hawwa* (*Eve*). A prolific writer, her literary output is varied and includes novels, plays, and hundreds of stories that have appeared in several volumes. The story "Half a Woman" ("Nisf Imra'a") is the title story of a collection published in Cairo in 1962.

Rafiqat al-Tabia Pseudonym for Zaynab Fahmi, a Moroccan fiction writer born in Casablanca in 1940. She is currently the head of a girls' school in Mohammedia. She writes in Arabic and has published three collections of short stories. The story "A Man and a Woman" ("Rajul wa Imra'a") is the title story of a collection published in

Casablanca in 1969. This is her first appearance in English.

Ghada Samman A leading poet and fiction writer, born in the Syrian village al-Shamiyya in 1942. Her father was first Rector of the University of Damascus, then Minister of Education. She obtained her B.A. in English literature from the University of Damascus. In 1964 she went to Lebanon and completed her M.A. at the American University in Beirut. She has worked as a translator, university lecturer, columnist, and journalist. She has written short stories, novels, poetry, and literary criticism. In 1977 she founded her own publishing company. In 1984 the Lebanese civil war forced her to leave Beirut for Paris, where she currently resides. Her works have been translated into a number of European languages. The story "Another Scarecrow" ("Faza' Tuyur Akhar") is from the collection *Layl al-Ghuraba'* (Beirut, 1966).

Khayriyya al-Saqqaf A Saudi short-story writer, born in Mecca in 1951. She received a bachelor's degree from the Girls' University College in Riyadh in 1973, and a master's degree from the University of Missouri in 1976. She has worked as editor of the women's section of the daily newspaper *Riyadh,* and as a lecturer at the Girls' University College. She writes articles and gives radio talks and public lectures. The story "The Second and the Truth" ("al-Thaniyya wa al-Haqiqa") is from the collection *An Tubhir nahwa al-Ab'ad* (Riyadh, 1982).

Sharifa al-Shamlan A Saudi writer, born in 1947. She studied journalism at the Girls' University College in Riyadh, from which she graduated in 1968. She currently works as the head of social services in the eastern part of her country. She has published short stories and

Biographical Notes

essays in various magazines. The story "Fragments from a Life" ("Maqati' min al-Haya") appeared in the Lebanese journal *al-Adab* (no. 4–6, April–June, 1987).

Sakina Fuad An Egyptian fiction writer, born in Port Said in 1944. She studied journalism at the University of Cairo and is currently the editor of the magazine *Radio and Television*, where she publishes critical reviews of Egyptian radio and television programs. She has published several volumes of short stories, many of which were made into film and television productions. The story "Pharaoh Is Drowning Again" ("al-Fir'un Yaghraq min Jadid") is from the collection *Millaf Qadiyyat Hubb* (Cairo, 1977). This is her first appearance in English.

Dalya Cohen-Mor, the translator of these stories, received her Ph.D. in Arabic language and literature from Georgetown University, Washington, D.C., and her M.A. in English language and literature from the State University of Utrecht, the Netherlands. She has lived and worked in the Middle East, Europe, and the United States. Her publications include *Yusuf Idris: Changing Visions* and *Yusuf Idris: The Piper Dies and Other Stories*. She is currently engaged in research into modern Arabic literature, with particular interest in the short story.